MW01285866

BY FANNIE FLAGG

Something to Look Forward To

The Wonder Boy of Whistle Stop

The Whole Town's Talking

The All-Girl Filling Station's Last Reunion

I Still Dream About You

Can't Wait to Get to Heaven

A Redbird Christmas

Standing in the Rainbow

Welcome to the World, Baby Girl!

Fannie Flagg's Original Whistle Stop Cafe Cookbook

Fried Green Tomatoes at the Whistle Stop Cafe

Daisy Fay and the Miracle Man
(originally published as *Coming Attractions*)

Something to Look Forward To

SOMETHING
TO LOOK
FORWARD TO

FANNIE FLAGG

RANDOM HOUSE

NEW YORK

Random House

An imprint and division of Penguin Random House LLC
1745 Broadway, New York, NY 10019
randomhousebooks.com
penguinrandomhouse.com

Copyright © 2025 by Willina Lane Productions, Inc.

Penguin Random House values and supports copyright. Copyright fuels creativity, encourages diverse voices, promotes free speech, and creates a vibrant culture. Thank you for buying an authorized edition of this book and for complying with copyright laws by not reproducing, scanning, or distributing any part of it in any form without permission. You are supporting writers and allowing Penguin Random House to continue to publish books for every reader. Please note that no part of this book may be used or reproduced in any manner for the purpose of training artificial intelligence technologies or systems.

RANDOM HOUSE and the HOUSE colophon are
registered trademarks of Penguin Random House LLC.

Hardback ISBN 9780593734414
Ebook ISBN 9780593734438

Printed in the United States of America on acid-free paper

2 4 6 8 9 7 5 3 1

First Edition

BOOK TEAM: Production editor: *Dennis Ambrose* • Managing editor: *Rebecca Berlant* •
Production manager: *Sandra Sjursen* • Copy editor: *Rachelle Mandik* •
Proofreaders: *Andrea Gordon, Caryl Weintraub,* and *Michael Burke*

The authorized representative in the EU for product safety and compliance
is Penguin Random House Ireland, Morrison Chambers, 32 Nassau Street,
Dublin D02 YH68, Ireland. https://eu-contact.penguin.ie.

In memory of

LEONA CHAPMAN FORTENBERRY

and

grandmothers, everywhere . . .

Preface

Dear Reader . . .

*If I may, just a short note before you begin. I just wanted
you to know that one of the great joys of my life has
always been observing other humans as they go about
living their daily lives. And as a result, I have become a
huge fan of the human being. Not only a fan but delighted
to be one myself, so thank you for always being just so
darn interesting and fun to watch!*

Sincerely,

Fannie Flagg

Fannie Flagg

Contents

Something to Look Forward To

Special Agent William Frawley

~≪≫~

He sat staring at his screen wondering what in the hell those humans were doing down there. Had they all gone completely nuts? The chief galactic observer on Planet 8676, who was in charge of observing the Milky Way Galaxy, shut down his screen and sent for his top agent.

"I have an assignment for you."

"Yes sir."

"I need a firsthand, up-close report, so I need to send you somewhere for a few weeks. Are you up for it?"

"Of course. Where do you want me to go?"

"Planet Earth. There's something weird going on there, and I can't figure it out. My heat-detection grid indicates large numbers of the human beings there are relocating themselves. I'm also detecting an inordinate number of spacecraft launchings outside of the planet's atmosphere. Earth is close to twenty-seven billion light-years away, so I'm unable to get a really detailed look, and I'm also noticing that a number of the human beings appear to be staring at their hands. Particularly in the country of America."

"Huh . . . that is weird."

"Agreed. So I need for you to go there and observe up-close, find out what it is they are looking at. In general, try to find out what the hell is going on."

"Yes sir."

He studied his screen again, then said, "On my image-map of that particular country, there are a lot of different regions, so maybe somewhere in their Midwest area."

"Fine."

"Okay, so I'll contact ICR and get you set up. Good luck."

"Thank you, sir."

The special agent then headed over to the Intergalactic Codes and Replicas Department to pick up his new form.

The head engineer greeted him and said, "I hear you are going to Planet Earth."

"Looks like."

He looked in his file. "Okay, intelligent life on Earth . . . Human beings. So, we need to make you up a human being form. Let's get started."

The special agent was curious. "What do human beings even look like?"

"Come on in the back and we'll scan some of them so you can see for yourself."

The agent was shown what they had on file pertaining to images of humans, of their politicians, various celebrities, entertainments, et cetera.

"Wow . . . humans are pretty funny-looking, huh?"

"Agreed. So, what would you prefer to be, male or female?"

"Oh gosh, I don't know . . . What do you think?"

"Male, I think. Might be easier. So which one of these male images would you prefer?"

The agent looked again. "Hmmm. How about that one?" he said, and pointed to a photo of Brad Pitt with his shirt off.

"I don't blame you, but that one might make it too hard for you to go unnoticed. The boss says you are there to observe, not to be observed."

"You're right. So I guess I need something more . . . average."

The head engineer then said, "Hey, how about that funny guy? He's on their *I Love Lucy* television show. He's married to a female human named Ethel. Fred Mertz, I think. Hold on." He brought up a clip of the TV show.

"Oh. Okay," said the special agent.

"William Frawley is the actor's name who plays the part of Fred. Is this one okay?"

"Sure, make me up to look something like that William Frawley. But maybe with a little more hair, and a little thinner . . . if you could?"

"You got it."

The special agent would be posing as a human only for a short while, but he already found himself getting a little vain about his looks. Oh well, he guessed that was just part of the territory.

At first, the replica department had some difficulty making the human eyes and knees work properly, but they soon solved the problem. So after the second go-round, the special agent entered the voice-activated finished replica form, and moments after stepping into the Superluminal Unit, Special Agent William Frawley appeared at the front desk of a Marriott hotel outside Fort Wayne, Indiana, and checked in. He showed them a small plastic card that had been put in his pocket, and they were all very nice and welcomed him. He liked his room, but now, being human, he was very tired and a little disoriented.

This was the first time he had ever encountered color. All the images of Earth on his boss's screen were light gray, but here on Earth, everything was a different color and it almost made him dizzy.

So he got a good night's sleep and prepared to start work the next day. The next morning, he went downstairs for a complimentary breakfast and ate something pink called a Pop-Tart, and drank some hot, brown liquid called coffee. Then he took a walk around the little town. It, too, was very colorful and very crowded with humans, and he was pleased that not one person who passed by seemed to notice that he was not one of them. In fact, most didn't even look at him.

But he could see right away that this was in part due to the odd behavior that had been recorded from his planet. He could see that the humans were not just looking at their hands, they were staring at things in their hands they called cellphones. All day and night it seemed they were busy looking at these cellphone things, sending messages and photos of themselves to other humans, and evidently other humans were sending some back.

He also spent a lot of time looking at the current news shows on all the different channels on a large TV screen. What a shock that was! All they seemed to report was bad news, and everybody had the most terrible things to say about other humans who did not agree with them. He purchased a cellphone and began studying what the man in the phone store called social media, read lots of blogs, and the same was true there. He also found out from the news that the launches his boss had seen were many satellites and the humans' attempt to expand their space travel. When he wasn't studying his TV screen and cellphone, he would just walk around town, go into a few bars and restaurants, and talk to people. He also observed that most of the humans he met had an opinion on everything and were happy to tell him what it was, even though he hadn't asked. And the interesting thing to him was they all believed that they were right. And many were quick to let him know that they had recently moved to the area so that they could talk to people who agreed with them. Others, who had differing opinions, had moved to another area of America, where they could talk to people who agreed with *them*. These humans seemed so odd. Quite a number of them, particularly the younger ones, had colored pictures and writing printed all over their arms and legs.

And a lot walked around town with some sort of four-legged animal on a string.

It was hard work, this observing humans all day long, but at night he really enjoyed himself, ordering room service and sitting up in bed, watching all the shows on the TV—particularly the old movie channel.

He was tickled when he saw pictures of what humans envisioned beings from other planets to look like. They thought aliens from outer space all had big, bulbous, bald heads and large black eyes. He had to laugh. He couldn't be sure about the others, but all the beings on his planet were about half the size of the tip of a needle, one hundred times smarter than humans, and perfectly formed. Most of the humans he was seeing were big and bulky, except for this one lady who worked at the Baskin-Robbins ice-cream parlor down the street from the hotel.

In his spare time, just to get a break from all the bad news on TV, he really enjoyed watching the old reruns of that *I Love Lucy* show on the classic TV channel. He loved seeing his namesake. It made him laugh to look at himself.

Never having been human, laughing was a new sensation for him, as were so many things. Before he came to Earth, Special Agent William Frawley had never had taste buds and never tasted coffee, or ever eaten food.

And he was finding the more he ate, the more he enjoyed it. Hamburgers, hot dogs, pizza, popcorn, fried chicken, and lately the special at Taco Bell. But he particularly loved ice cream and was soon at the Baskin–Robbins ice-cream parlor every afternoon at four.

At this point, he really had all the information he needed, and could have gone home to his planet, but he was having such a good time, he decided to stay just a little longer. And it wasn't just the ice cream he liked at Baskin–Robbins, it was the lady behind the counter.

He supposed she was about his replica's age, and she was as sweet as the product she sold. Her name was Debbie, and she seemed to like him too. After a while they had a routine going. Each afternoon when he came in, she would say, "Bill, we need to find your favorite, so today I want you to try Pralines and Cream." By the end of the first month, he had gone through all thirty-one flavors, from Chocolate Mint Chip, Cherries Jubilee, and Lemon Sorbet to Chocolate-Chip Cookie Dough. He made his decision and declared nothing beat just plain Vanilla. "Good choice," said Debbie. "I agree."

Along with the fabulous sensation of tasting that sweet, cold, and creamy ice cream at the end of a hot afternoon, he suddenly started feeling something else. He didn't know what it was—they didn't have feelings where he came from—but he felt something warm and pleasant in his chest area as he sat in the corner and watched his new friend, Debbie, scoop up ice cream for the other customers. He couldn't get over how pretty she was. He liked the way she smiled at everybody. Later he found out she was a widow, with a grown son who lived out of town. He told her he was in town doing research for a big tech company.

One day she invited him to her home for dinner. She said, "Bill, you need to get out of that hotel for a change."

Debbie lived in a little redbrick house that was neat and clean, and when he walked in he was surprised to see that there was a live animal living inside. It was called a cat.

The minute Bill sat down, a big fluffy, gray stripey thing jumped up on his lap and started pushing its paws back and forth on his leg.

Debbie said, "Oh Bill, Mr. Tubbs likes you. He's making biscuits."

Bill enjoyed being there and enjoyed learning how to clean the dishes they had just used. But most of all he enjoyed the feeling he had being inside a real human home.

Soon, he was at Debbie's for dinner every Friday night. Then when she went to visit her son's new baby in South Dakota, she asked him if he would stay at her place and look after her cat while she was gone. He was happy to do it. The hotel room was getting a little old. When she came back, she showed him photos of her new human grandbaby. It was bald and had big eyes. How funny.

He was having such a wonderful time on Earth, so much to see, so many fun things to do. A fellow named Phil, whom he met at the ice-cream parlor, had even taken him outside the city to play golf.

They did not have large bodies of water on his planet, and one of the other things he really enjoyed was swimming. He had made friends with the lifeguard at the YMCA pool and was, at present, learning the backstroke. And afterward there was ice cream. But the time had come for him to get back home to his planet, and he hated to leave. He knew he would really miss Debbie and the friends he had made. And the cat. He would miss that silly cat. But he had a job to do, and the boss was waiting for his report.

The following week, he said goodbye to Debbie, petted the cat, and had one more double scoop of vanilla ice cream. The next morning Mr. William Frawley checked out of the hotel and left no forwarding address.

He arrived back on Planet 8676 in less than a second, but for the first few hours, he still had a lingering sadness as he looked around at his gray planet. It seemed so . . . gray. He supposed in time he would get over missing

Debbie, and her cat. Sadly there were no animals here, and he would love to have a cat. But knowing he would never see Debbie was the hardest part. He realized now he might have been a little bit in love with her and didn't know it.

But as ordered, he immediately reported back to the Intergalactic Codes and Replicas Department. He was greeted by the head engineer. "Welcome back. How was your trip? Any problems with the replica form?"

"No, not really, it seemed to fit in perfectly. I don't think anybody ever guessed I wasn't real."

"Good. Okay, so let's remove the form and get you over to the boss. I know he's waiting."

After the special agent was removed from his replica form, he looked at it lying on the table and said, "So long, Bill," as he watched it being deflated, folded up, and put in a drawer with all the others labeled "Human. Male. Earth."

When he entered the main office, his boss was scanning his screen and looked up. "Well, first of all, glad you're back safe and sound. So tell me, why are the human beings looking at their hands?"

"Oh, right, sir. It's not their hands, it's a flat, metal device they all have called a cellphone. They use it to communicate with each other."

"Oh, okay. Well, that explains it. Hmm."

"But boss, if you don't mind, before I get to the rest of my report, I have to tell you something really interesting about Earth that I don't think any of us knew. Once you get there, it's not gray like it is on your screen."

"It isn't?" The boss looked back at his screen and said, "That's what it looks like from here."

"I know, but they have something down there. Color. Everything there is a different color."

"A different color?"

"It's hard to explain, but there are distinct wavelengths of bright, vivid color. And not just one shade, like blue or green. You should see the trees. They are all different shades of green. Pale green, dark green, lime green, sometimes all on one tree. And they have flowers. Pink and yellow and purple, red, you name it. It's the most amazing thing. And by the way, my favorite color was yellow. My friend Debbie has a white fence that's covered with little yellow roses. I wish you could have seen it. And they have this round fruit thing called an orange that is really the color called orange. And all the rivers and the lakes are all kinds of different colors of blue and green. Even the cat. The cat was gray, but it wasn't a solid gray, it was all shades and stripes of dark gray and light gray."

The boss had no idea what he was talking about, and wondered if maybe this agent had been compromised or had his currents altered while he was on Earth.

The special agent was also wondering, What's wrong with me?

Maybe shooting through space so fast while he still had human emotions had kicked something off, because he couldn't seem to stop talking.

"And boss, all the birds there are so many colors. Redbirds, bluebirds. You can't believe it. I saw a peacock at the zoo that had at least a hundred different colors. On just one bird! And you should see this little ladybug. It's bright red with black polka dots. And also, humans have something called smell."

"Not familiar."

"They smell things as they inhale, through their noses. Things there have a fragrance. The flowers, the grass, all have a fresh smell. And they also have food that they put in their mouths at least three times a day for fuel. Delicious, by the way. But I mentioned cats . . . I really wish we had cats here," he said wistfully.

"What's a cat?"

"I couldn't begin to tell you. Cats are a real piece of work. I kept my friend Debbie's cat for two weeks, and when he wasn't ripping furniture, he was a lot of fun to pet. And when they're happy they purr. He would sleep right by my head." He sighed. "I know we are so much smarter than humans and have a more advanced civilization, but it's amazing what humans can do. For instance, they can take a blank piece of canvas, look at something, and paint a picture of it. And they can sing and dance and invent songs. Right out of their heads. I don't know how they do it. A lot of them are serious, but a lot are silly, too; they are always doing things to make other people laugh, sometimes they even laugh at themselves."

"Really?"

"Yes, and they have a lot of things down there that are really a lot of fun. Hamburgers, hot dogs, ice cream, swimming. Oh, and golf. It's a game played on soft, green grass. And let me tell you, it looks easy, but it's not. And get this. At night you look up and you can see the Earth's one big moon. Oh, and the trees. Some trees make these little wooden things called pinecones, and they're perfectly shaped. I wish I could have brought one back."

The boss looked at his watch.

"Oh, sorry I'm so talkative, boss. I guess I'm still a little wound up from the trip."

"Well, it sounds like you got a lot of good information. Did you happen to find out what all the launches are about?"

"Oh that, yes. They are doing a lot of new experimentation with what to them is more advanced space travel."

"Space travel, huh?"

"Yes, and the human relocations are a result of their desire to move to a place where they all agree with one another. All you read or hear about on their news shows is who hates who, and how unhappy everyone is."

The boss said, "I don't understand. If everything on Earth is as beautiful and wonderful as you say, then why are the humans not enjoying it more? What is the reason that they're all so unhappy?"

"That's the strange thing, boss. Some of them are very happy and having a great time down there."

"Hmmmm. Yes, that is odd." The boss thought a moment and said, "Listen, I need a little time to scan a few more items pertaining to human behavior that I may have missed. So why don't you go and get a little rest and we'll continue with the briefing later on this afternoon. Okay?"

"Yes sir."

"But I must say, from what you've told me so far, these human being creatures are a lot more complicated than I thought."

To be continued . . .

Beware of Weathermen

Sally Gordon had always been ambitious. When other fifteen-year-old girls had posters of teen heartthrobs on their bedroom walls, she had pictures of Diane Sawyer and Barbara Walters. Sally's dream was to one day become a famous news reporter.

Now forty-eight years old, Sally woke up in a nondescript hotel room in Milwaukee, Wisconsin, at four A.M. She had to be at the TV station by 5 A.M. for hair and makeup, ready to go on-air, anchoring the 6 A.M. news, followed by the noon news, and finish up with the 6 P.M. nightly report.

She had just started her new job three days ago, and this morning she wondered how many more times in her life she could start over. She didn't know if she had another start-over left. It was getting harder and harder.

This time she was starting over back in Milwaukee, Wisconsin, the exact town where she had begun her television career twenty-eight years ago. Granted, at a different station and on a bigger salary, but the same town. At this point she was so tired of starting a new job, having to be pleasant, and getting to know new people. But she got up to face another long day anyway.

Later, after the morning news show, as Sally was headed out the door to go look for an apartment, Mary, who worked the station's switchboard, handed her a message and said, "Miss Gordon, this lady, Roberta, just called, and said she needed to get in touch with you as soon as possible, regarding someone you used to work with, a John Patrick Finnley?"

Sally winced. Oh damn, that was a name she'd hoped to never have to hear again in this lifetime.

"Did she say what it was about?"

"No, she just left her number and to call her."

Sally sighed. That was the problem with being on television. People always knew where and how to find you. She went back to her office, sat down, and thought about what she should do. It was not just a name from her past. It was a reminder of one of the worst times in her life, including being in the trenches, covering wars and natural disasters all over the world. And now, just as she was getting settled, John had to show up again. What was he doing here?

She had been told he had left Milwaukee years ago and moved to New Mexico or Arizona. Other than that, she had no idea what he had been doing or where he had been for the past twenty-eight years. And more important, she didn't want to know. But now she was stuck.

She couldn't pretend she didn't get the message, and she didn't want to be rude to the daughter. And so after going back and forth about what to do, she finally figured she might as well bite the bullet and get it over with. She dialed the number. She just hoped to God he wouldn't try to get together again. Then she would really have to be rude.

After a few rings, a woman answered. "Hello."

"Hi, is this Roberta?"

"Yes, this is Roberta."

"This is Sally Gordon."

"Oh, yes! Oh, thank you, I'm so glad you called. You don't know me but I feel like I know you. Daddy talked about you all the time and about how much fun you guys used to have when you worked together at the station."

"Oh really?"

"Yes, and I just couldn't believe when I saw you on the news this morning."

They were even. Sally couldn't believe John had a daughter . . . considering. "Yes, I just started a few days ago."

"I know, we used to follow your career everywhere, and here you are back again. How great is that?"

"Yes, here I am. And . . . so, ah . . . how is John?"

"Daddy?"

"Yes, how's he's doing?"

"Oh . . . Daddy's dead."

"What?"

"Daddy died over two months ago."

Sally was stunned. This news was totally unexpected, to say the least. "Oh, I'm so sorry . . . I hadn't heard."

"Yes, he passed away back in March . . . Anyhow, the reason I was calling was to let you know his memorial service is this coming Tuesday. We put it off because of the holidays, and it's a graveside service so we wanted to wait until it warmed up a little bit."

Sally was still in a state of shock but managed to say, "I see."

"So I hope you can come. I know you must be busy, but it would mean so much to us if you could. It's going to be at Sunrise Gardens, section six at eleven thirty A.M. We could have someone pick you up if you like."

"No, no, that won't be necessary."

"Well, it shouldn't be too hard to find us. As you come in the front gate, turn right at the fountain. You can't miss it."

"Okay, um . . . I'll try my best."

"Oh, do. Like I said, it will mean so much to me and Mother. And maybe now that you are back in town, we can all get to be friends. I know that would have made Daddy so happy."

"Okay then, well, thank you for the call."

After she hung up, Sally could've kicked herself for calling. Now she was in a real quandary. Oh God, just what she didn't want. To be friends with John's wife. Or his second, third, or fourth, for all she knew. Or go down that memory lane and talk about John . . . to anyone. She did not want to remember how he had absolutely broken her heart. But no matter how much pain he had caused her, she could never be happy that anyone was dead. On the other hand, at least he would not be trying to get together.

She had only been twenty-one when they met. She had just graduated from Northwestern University, where she'd majored in theatre and communications, when the father of her best friend saw her do the part of Ado Annie in the musical *Oklahoma* and offered her a summer job at his television station in Milwaukee as a co-hostess of their local morning show.

At the time, John had been the big local sports-and-weatherman, and the most popular on-air personality. Everybody loved John. On Easter he would do his weather report wearing a bunny costume, and at Christmas he would show up in his elf outfit. He was also Jo-Jo the Clown on the four-o'clock children's show and appeared as Jo-Jo at birthday parties and conventions all over town. No question about it, he had that devilish charm and twinkle in his eye, and it didn't hurt that he had brown, curly hair and was as cute and as funny as could be.

And from the minute Sally came to work at the station, he wasted no time in sweeping her off her feet. At first she was flattered; she was new in town and the most popular guy in town was chasing her. And he did make her laugh at some of his antics. Although she swore to herself that she would never get serious about a guy, and always put her career first, before she knew it she was madly in love. Who wouldn't be? And John was her first real love. But as much as she wanted to, as Doris Day sang, "Shout it from the highest hills," she couldn't tell anyone. The station had a rule against on-air personalities dating, so they had to keep their romance a secret. It was so hard.

Everyone in town knew John. He couldn't go anywhere without people calling out to him, and soon everyone began to recognize her as the morning-show girl. But she was in love, so everything about it was exciting. Even the sneaking around and meeting in secret places. John had once dressed up as an old lady, and they had gone to dinner, right out in public. What a character!

It wasn't until later that she discovered that John had a history of sweeping a lot of girls off their feet, many of whom were married women. One woman had even been the wife of their station boss. And she only found this out because one night the woman had burst into her apartment, screaming terrible things, and had thrown a pair of shoes at John, barely missing his head. After the woman stormed out, John tried to deny they were his shoes, but they were clearly Jo-Jo the Clown's shoes. To make matters worse, he got mad at Sally for not locking her door.

Things had not gone well after that; the irate wife had sent Sally information in the mail about John's past. It seems he had been fired from two other stations for getting two different weathergirls pregnant.

When Sally had confronted him about it, he said the girls had been lying. And even if it was true, it wasn't his fault. He had warned them he didn't want kids. He said he couldn't help it if women were always coming after him, and he'd only got involved because he hadn't wanted to hurt their feelings. As he talked, Sally realized something she was not wanting to face: he was lying to her. But it was too late. She was too hopelessly in love with him to even think about leaving him. It would be too painful. Her only hope now was that one day he would settle down and change. She was even willing to give up her dreams of a career just to have him.

But finally, after a few more incidents, the straw that broke the camel's back came when the new station manager got word that John had been seen going in and out of Sally's apartment at all hours of the night. John had completely denied it. He said that it wasn't him, that Sally was having an affair with some other man who just looked like him. Thanks to his lies, and the station manager's fear of a local scandal, she was the one who wound up getting fired.

So when she got an offer from the big television station in Atlanta, she jumped at it. And before she was able to pack up and get out of town, she heard John was already romancing the new girl. The weasel.

Now she was torn about what to do about the phone

call. Why couldn't they have buried him just a little bit sooner? Now she was damned if she went to the service, and damned if she didn't. If she did go, there was a slight chance she might run into people she didn't want to see. But on the other hand, if she didn't go, John's daughter could tell everyone on Facebook or wherever, and she'd wind up looking bad in a new town. People love to gossip. And after all, they had worked together for only a short while. She wondered whether length of acquaintance counted where funerals were concerned. Oh God, she didn't know a thing about funeral protocol.

That night she called her longtime friend Nanette in Chicago and asked her advice.

Nanette said, "Sally, I know you. You'll just feel guilty if you don't go, so you might as well go and get it over with."

"Yeah . . . so . . . you think it's the right thing to do?"

"I think so. John may have been a bastard, but the daughter can't help that. Besides, you've done harder things than this. You covered the Iraq war for God's sake."

"I know, but I'd feel like such a phony, pretending to mourn someone that—"

"Listen, you think that's hard? Try going to your mother-in-law-from-hell's funeral. You know what a mama's boy Ted is, so I couldn't very well break out in song, like I wanted to. So we all have to do it at some time. Call me and let me know how it goes, okay?"

And so, after a few days of going back and forth, she finally decided to take Nanette's advice and go to the darn thing. After all, it would only be a couple of hours of her time at the most. Thank heavens for Nanette's help. Sally could report a news story like nobody's business, but she struggled with how to do real life. What should she wear? After all, she wasn't the grieving widow, thank God. The morning of the memorial, after going through almost all her wardrobe trying to figure out what would be proper, she finally settled on a dark-brown turtleneck sweater, black skirt, and a camel-colored coat. She examined herself in the mirror and added a small strand of pearls to the ensemble. She would show up at the last minute, right before 11:30, just in time to be seen, do a quick hello to the daughter, and leave as soon as she could without being rude.

She drove in through the cemetery gates and turned right at the fountain, but she was not quite sure where section six was. Thankfully she saw the small white funeral signs with arrows that had been put out, pointing the way.

In a few minutes she found it and saw the group of people gathered at the gravesite. She parked her car and sat and waited until around 11:28, then walked over to the site and quickly scanned the crowd. She then noticed a young woman standing on the side who seemed to be the one greeting everyone as they came up to her. She asked an older lady if the young woman in the black hat was the daughter and was told that she was. Sally then quietly walked over and stood in line. When her turn came, she approached her and said, "Sally Gordon, I just wanted to say hello."

The woman did not recognize her at first, then said, "Oh yes, Miss Gordon, hello."

"Hello, and I want to tell you how sorry I am for your loss."

The young woman reached out and took her hand and squeezed it and seemed genuinely touched to see her. "Oh, thank you so much for coming. It's so kind of you."

Sally then stepped aside to let the others who were behind her move forward. Good. She had made her presence known. She then pretended to see someone she knew and waved as she made her way to the back row of white chairs that had been set up for the service, and quickly sat down. She looked back to find her car and noted exactly where it was, so that right after the service was over, she could head straight to it.

She didn't want to have to wander around looking for it and take the chance of running into people who wanted to chat.

As she sat there, she was a little surprised at the size of the crowd. At 11:35 a few people were still arriving.

A moment later, a nice-looking older man stood beside her and said, "Pardon me, is that seat taken?" She looked at the empty seat beside her and shook her head.

"May I?"

He sat down and said, "I'm Richard, by the way, long-time friend of John and Anna's."

"Ah, I'm Sally."

He nodded quickly and whispered, "Yes, I know who you are."

She gave him a quick little smile back and looked straight ahead.

Oh God, she had no idea what John might have told this man about her; he was such a liar. And the last thing she wanted to do was chitty-chat, so she quickly picked up her purse and pretended she was looking for something. The man evidently got the message and did not continue to engage her in conversation.

As she sat waiting for the service to begin, watching the daughter still greeting people, she was suddenly hit with a wave of sadness. Not about John being dead. She suddenly realized that if things had turned out differently, the nice young woman might have been her own daughter.

After she had left Milwaukee, her life had been spent moving from one network job to the next, running around the world, chasing one breaking story after another. Along the way, there had been other men, but nothing permanent. Her personal life had mostly been a mess, but career-wise, she had reached her goal. After her news career in Atlanta, she had quickly shot up the ladder, going from one top job to the next, and at one time had been one of the most sought-after female news anchors in the business, winning award after award and being recognized all over the world. But at forty-eight, she was not as sought-after as she once had been. One by one, younger girls in short dresses and high heels were being brought in to replace her. She had begun slowly slipping back down the ladder, step by lonely step.

After having worked at the top network- and cable-news outlets, covering the news from all over the world, she was now covering only the greater Milwaukee area, right back where she had started, too young to retire and too old for advancement.

Her thoughts were suddenly interrupted when the minister stepped up to the podium and rang a small bell to indicate they were ready to begin the service. People quickly went to their seats as the minister began by offering the family condolences, and spoke directly to Anna, the wife, who was sitting in the middle of the front row. Sally was again surprised when she saw whom the minister was addressing. Anna was a lovely looking gray-haired woman, all in black of course, who was clearly devastated at her loss. John had obviously done well in choosing her. Sally had expected someone a little younger and a little bit more flashy; he always went for the good-looking blondes, the kind she used to be.

As the minister continued his tribute to John and, as he put it, "A tribute to a life well lived," Sally had to admit that in hearing all the good things about John, she was impressed. According to the minister, John had been an ideal husband, father, and now grandfather of four. She looked again at the wife and suspected she'd had a lot to do with that. Something had turned him around. The way the minister had talked, John and Anna had obviously been longtime members of the church. She had heard about people who had experienced some sort of spiritual epiphany and had turned their lives completely around. And if that was what had happened to John, she envied him. For a long time now she had been secretly wishing for something like that to happen to her. Some kind of miracle that could make her feel alive again. The minister seemed so nice. Maybe now that she would be here for a while, she should try to join a church. Take a stab at being a normal human being.

As she listened to more and more of the tribute, she had to smile. John may have been a serious churchgoer and upstanding citizen, but he must have kept just a little bit of his sense of humor. People laughed at the funny stories the minister told about him, his frustration at not being able to play golf well, and the way he would react when he missed a shot. Of course, she knew that they aways gilded the lily a bit when talking about the deceased, and, for the sake of the family, left all the bad stuff out. But still, the fact that so many of his friends showed up was a sign that some of the high praise must be true.

At the end of the service, before the actual interment, the minister announced that people who wished to do so were invited to come up and throw a handful of dirt in the small square hole where the box of ashes would be lowered. The perfect time to leave. The man sitting beside her evidently had the same idea and got up and walked in the direction of the cars. He said, "Very nice service, don't you think?"

She nodded. "Oh yes, very nice."

"If you don't mind me asking, how did you know John?" Sally was glad to know he seemed not to know the details of the relationship.

"Oh," she said. "I met him through work. A long time ago, though . . ."

"Ah . . . I see."

She reached her car and said, "Nice meeting you," then opened her car door and got in before he could ask any more questions. He was perfectly nice, but a bit talky.

As she drove back to the station, she kept thinking about John's funeral. Maybe if she had not left him when she did, and he had gotten his act together sooner, she would have married him. And that really could have been her sitting there today surrounded by so many nice friends and family. She might have had a family, and a real home. The minister had talked on and on about John and Anna's beautiful house and all the wonderful Christmas parties and backyard barbecues they had. Damn John anyway. How was she to know that one day he would wind up becoming a decent human being after all? The bastard. And even sadder, how was she to know that fame and success was not what it was cracked up to be? Yes, she'd had all the awards and accolades. How was she to know she would wind up feeling so alone, even in a room full of strangers?

Her only consolation was that people always said that things turn out the way they are supposed to. But she was starting to not believe it. She had been the one who had been famous, but John was the one who had obviously wound up having a happy life, with so many friends and family who clearly loved him.

At this point in her life, Sally doubted if anybody would show up at her funeral. She hadn't been in one place long enough to make long-lasting friends. Probably Nanette would come, but would anyone else? After the service, she spent a long night feeling sorry for herself, and if it wouldn't have made her face and eyes so puffy, she would have had a few of those little bottles of vodka in the little hotel fridge.

. . .

The next morning, after the 6 A.M. news was over, Mary buzzed Sally on the intercom and said, "Hey hon, that gal Roberta just called back and wanted to give you more details about the memorial service today. She said if she didn't reach you, there would be signs pointing the way so you shouldn't have any trouble finding them."

"What? Is she kidding? I just saw her yesterday." She buzzed back, "Mary, do me a favor and call the cemetery. Find out if the John Finnley service was yesterday. I know it was, I was there."

The daughter had seemed so nice, so normal, but she must be some sort of a crackpot.

A few minutes later, Mary buzzed her back. "I hate to tell you, hon, but it's today at eleven thirty. The service you went to yesterday was for somebody named John Hornbeck."

"What?"

"Yep, that's what the gal said."

Oh my God, she had been at some complete stranger's memorial service!

Had she gotten the day mixed up? Roberta had said Monday, hadn't she? Or had she said Tuesday?

Oh, how embarrassing! What must those people have thought? No wonder she didn't know anybody. And no wonder they seemed surprised to see her.

She quickly got on the internet and looked up obits for March and finally found it:

JOHN PATRICK FINNLEY 1954–2016.

Mr. Finnley died on March 12, after a short illness. He is survived by three wives and one daughter, Roberta Finnley, a longtime resident of Phoenix, where he was residing at the time of his death.

Sally quickly checked her watch. It was early enough, so she rushed back to the hotel, changed into yesterday's memorial clothes, and headed out. She would only be able to stay a minute, but she could at least say hello to Roberta. She followed the same little white funeral signs, again. When she reached the same spot as yesterday, she was surprised to see nothing there but a few people sitting at a portable picnic table, drinking Pabst Blue Ribbon beer.

Sally got out and walked up to the woman in the black tank top, who said she was Roberta, and she was introduced to a few of her friends from the tattoo parlor where she worked. "See, I told you daddy knew somebody famous!" As it turned out, Roberta was a large, friendly woman whose entire left arm was covered with a portrait of Waylon Jennings. A conversation piece, to say the least. She said, "I'm so glad you showed up, Sally. Can we get a picture with you? Nobody's gonna believe I know you, I'm gonna put it up on the wall at work. And by the way, anytime you want a tattoo, it's on the house. You being such a close friend of Daddy's. Momma's sorry she couldn't come, but she got hit with the shingles again.

She said to say hello. Me and Tony are headed over to Arizona to clear out Daddy's things from the trailer. It's in foreclosure, so we only have thirty days to do it."

Poor John. She found out from Roberta that he had not had an easy life. She said that with his reputation with the women and all, he was never able to get back into television and wound up just drifting around the country, selling used cars, marrying different women, and had been sued for child support so often that he'd spent some time in jail. It was sad, but one thing Roberta said made Sally feel better. She said, "Oh Daddy was a rascal all right, but you know, Sally, he always could make you laugh, right up to the end."

When she got back to the station, she thought about calling Mrs. John Hornbeck and apologizing for crashing her husband's funeral, but she decided not to and was glad she hadn't. Four days later she received the loveliest note from her.

Dear Ms. Gordon,

Just a short note to thank you for honoring our John by your presence at his service on Sunday. I am sorry I did not have a chance to say hello, and hope if there is ever anything you need, in your return to our city, you'll feel free to call on us.

Sincerely,
Mrs. John Hornbeck

Several weeks later, Sally received a surprise phone call from Richard, the man who had sat by her at the Hornbeck service. He said, "Ms. Gordon, I hope I'm not being too bold, but I was wondering if I might take you to dinner some night?"

Not too long after that first dinner, Sally quit her job and later married Richard, who was the president of a large bank with many branches. As it turned out, Richard Johnson was a widower, with three daughters and seven grandchildren, with two more on the way.

And as for Sally, there was no more getting up at four in the morning, no more hair and makeup, living in hotels and bad apartments, eating frozen dinners. She now had a lovely home, a new church, new friends, and a new family who all just adored her. And all because she went to the wrong funeral. So maybe things really do turn out the way they are supposed to.

Darla Womble

POT LUCK, ARKANSAS
2004

At 9:18 A.M., in and around Pot Luck, Arkansas, thirty-eight relatives of Darla Ann Womble received a frantic email, which read:

DARLA'S NOT DEAD, AND SHE'S MAD AS HELL!

After seeing the email, two people threw up, one fainted, and another decided he would run for his life. This news came as quite a shock to all, especially since all thirty-eight had recently attended the reading of Darla's "Last Will and Testament."

It had all started on July 14 when sixty-six-year-old Darla Womble, a widow and recently retired English teacher, had not shown up at the Wednesday-night Pot Luck Methodist church dinner. That night many people had remarked that it was not like Darla to miss it. She had said on many occasions that as long as she didn't have to cook, she would be there. And so after Darla had not returned any of her phone calls or answered any of her emails, Sissy Womble, her first cousin Wade Womble's wife, drove over to Darla's redbrick ranch home and found it was locked and empty, but her car was still in the garage. Sissy also noticed that Darla's prize gardenia bushes had not been watered. This was certainly not like Darla. She was religious about her watering.

Also there was dust on her windowsills. Darla would not have allowed that. She was as vain about her house as she was about her looks. She never stepped out her door unless she was fully made up, and fully dressed in the latest fashions. Something was definitely wrong.

Sissy went home and immediately reported this to the local authorities.

When Sheriff Lamar Jenkins heard the report, he too was alarmed. He went over to her house and found the same thing. Dust, plus leaves on her sidewalk. This was not like Darla at all. She was as regular as clockwork, and one of the most responsible citizens in town. Her home was as neat and clean as her classroom had been. She would never have just walked out without at least asking someone to sweep her sidewalk and water her prize gardenias.

And so, after Darla had been missing for over three days, Sheriff Lamar Jenkins announced that a search for her was to begin.

Everyone was shocked. Pot Luck was a small town, and most all the people in the area of town where Darla lived had been a member of the Womble family, either a Womble by birth or married to a Womble.

The Wombles never seemed to move anywhere else. And considering the stupid behavior and lack of common sense of some of the Wombles, Jenkins had suspected inbreeding. That was a gene pool headed straight to the nut house or the penitentiary. Over the years, he had dealt with enough Wombles to last a lifetime. What kind of idiot would drive through a car wash in a 1963 Ford convertible with the top down, or light a stick of dynamite and then put it in their back pocket? The sheriff really had no use for any of the Wombles, except for one, and as far as he was concerned, the only sane one in the bunch. The truth was that Lamar had always been just a little bit in love with Darla. They had gone all through Pot Luck Grammar School and High School together, and although they both had married other people, they had remained good friends. Just another reason Lamar had no use for the Wombles. He didn't like the way they used Darla, always hitting her up for cash. They'd been taking advantage of her for years, ever since she had received her husband Ferland's rather large life-insurance settlement. Ferland had been a roofer by trade, and had tripped over a Diet Dr Pepper can someone had left, and fallen off the roof of the county courthouse.

Meanwhile, the search for Darla went on. And Monday afternoon, much to Lamar's regret, what was thought to be Darla Womble's burned remains were discovered in a shallow grave in her own backyard, not more than twenty feet from her home. Foul play was suspected.

But who would have wanted to kill Darla? It was a good question, since most of her relatives owed her money and would be just as happy to not have to pay her back.

Upon hearing the news of the remains being found, her first cousin Wade Womble's first thought was a question: Did she leave a will, and am I in it? The minute he put down the phone, he ran out the door, ready to hightail it over to Darla's house as fast as he could.

As he ran down the steps, his wife, Sissy, called out after him, "And get the jewelry!" He jumped in his truck and gunned it. He wanted to get there first, before the other relatives had a chance to beat him to it. When he got to Darla's house, he slipped under the yellow crime-scene tape and found that the doors were still locked, so he ran around and jimmied open the back door, then went through the entire place until he finally found what he was looking for. Darla's will. It had been in a kitchen drawer, underneath the operating instructions for her brand-new microwave oven. He grabbed the paper, ran out, and headed home. As he was leaving he passed several of the other relatives who were headed to Darla's as well.

When he got back to their trailer, his wife was waiting. "Well? Did you get the jewelry?"

"Naw, I forgot. But I did find the will."

"Oh good. Did we get anything?"

He threw it on the table in disgust. "She has it divided between all of us," he said, and he flopped down in his army-green velveteen recliner. Sissy threw her hands up in the air. "Oh, for God's sake, I knew it. I told you, didn't I tell you? God darn it. We've been waiting all this time, and for almost nothing. She shoulda left us more. I could just kill her."

"Yeah, well, yer a little late. Somebody beat you to it."

"Do you think Arnelle and Naylon did it?"

"Nope, I still think it was Darryl Jr. He's always having a fit to get his hands on her Mustang. He done stole it twice. Darla hadn't been missing but a couple of days and he was already in it, running it up and down the road. But we all had a motive, I guess. Or it could have been Lucille. She was always wanting to move into Darla's house."

Sissy said, "Well, I want that sofa and chairs in her living room, I know that. And the microwave."

"Yeah, but you know Lucille is gonna fight you tooth-and-nail for it. She's gonna try and get everything she can get her grubby little hands on."

"Well, we deserve to get most of it, having to bow and scrape to Darla, thinking she was better than us. She thought she was so smart, just because she went to that teachers' college. She got all above herself, didn't she? Well, look at her now. You could put all of what's left of her in an envelope. Still, I was countin' on some dental implants. Now I'm shit outta luck."

Wade said, "Maybe not. Ain't nobody seen that will yet."

"But did anybody sign it as a witness? They'd know about it."

He looked at the piece of paper. "Nope . . . all it says is, 'My last will and testament. I will all my worldly goods to be divided evenly among my surviving relatives,' signed Darla Ann Womble Carter."

Wade then looked at his wife with a sly smile. "So, I'll tell you what I'm gonna do. I'm just gonna tear it up and flush it down the toilet. That's what. So you still might have a chance for them teeth yet."

Sissy smiled at her husband. "You're so smart. Now I know why I married you."

"It wadn' for my good looks?"

She slapped him playfully on the shoulder. "You silly fool, hand it to me. I'm gonna put it in a pan in the oven, burn it up, then sling the ashes out in the trash bin."

After all the suspects had been questioned, and no arrests had been made, Wade, anxious to get on with it, announced that the family ought to get together and decide how to go about executing Darla's last wishes and plan the memorial service. He said they should all meet at Darla's house at the end of the week. On the day of the meeting, there was to be a reading of the will. Distant relatives they had not seen in a while and some they had never met showed up.

After they all settled in, Wade got up and spoke. "Good to see y'all. Sorry it had to be this way, and I know you all have come far and wide for a reading of the will, but after an extensive search, I can tell you for a fact there ain't no will, so we will have to figure out where to go from here. But first thing y'all should know is that Darla told Sissy and me that we was gettin' the house."

Lucille Wilson, Darla's second cousin, stood up. "Well I don't care what you say, Wade. She promised to leave *me* the house."

"Do you have that in writing?"

"No . . ."

"Sit down."

"I'm not sittin' down. I worked my fingers to the bone taking care of her when she come down with that bad case of pneumonia, and I wouldn't have done if I didn't think she was gonna put me in her will. You know damn well I wouldn't have." She then turned and looked at the crowd. "And where was any of you, when she was sick?"

"Sit down, Lucille," said Sissy. "You're a damned liar. All you ever did was badmouth her behind her back, and I know for a fact that you're the one who stole her watch when she was down with that pneumonia."

"You slut. She gave me that watch!"

"Uh-huh, sure she did. That's another lie, and don't think when all that money went missing that everybody didn't know it was you that took it."

"You're a liar."

"Then where the hell would you ever get enough money to buy yourself that designer purse?" asked Sissy.

"I got it at the outlet mall on sale, that's where I got it. Besides, I didn't steal that money. I earned it, and she was just too cheap to pay me what I was worth."

Suddenly Bernice, who had once been married to Darla's third cousin Donny Womble, stood up and in a loud voice announced, "Now that she's dead, I am finally free to tell the truth. She did not want you to know this, but Darla and I have been secret lovers for the past twenty years, and she told me that if anything ever happened to her she wanted me to have her house."

There was a moment of dead silence until Bernice's present husband, Alford, said, "Oh, sit down, Bernice, nobody's gonna believe that." So she sat down. Of course it was a lie, but she thought she might give it a try anyway.

Someone else then asked if anybody knew if Darla had a savings account and how could they find out?

"And how come Darryl Jr. got the car? Who said he could have it, and where is he?" said another.

"I've got dibs on her dishes," said a third. "Y'all can take the pots and pans."

"Well, I want the flat-screen TV," said Ruby Womble.

"I do too . . ."

And on and on it went, until Wade said, "All right, all right, everybody settle down . . . Okay, for the television, heads or tails? Flip. Heads."

"Tails!" yelled Lucille.

"The tails take the television."

Then Darla's niece Alice, who had come all the way from Little Rock, raised her hand.

Wade said, "What is it you want, Alice?"

"I don't want anything. I just came because I thought this was going to be about Aunt Darla, and how sorry we are about what happened. I loved her. And I want to find out who did this terrible thing to her, not to fight over who gets what."

Sissy asked her, "So you don't want anything?"

"No. I don't want anything."

"Okay then," said Wade, "everybody come get what you want. The sheriff's gonna be here in less than an hour to lock the place up."

After that announcement, people jumped up and started running all through Darla's home, opening drawers, taking what they wanted, trying on her clothes, taking pictures off the wall, towels, washcloths . . . and Jay Jr., the pothead, ran and grabbed all the medicine out of her medicine chest before anyone else could get there. And the rest of the afternoon was not pretty. Gladys got into a fistfight out in the yard with Sissy over the microwave oven and had one of her front teeth knocked out.

After the place had been picked bone-dry, including all the toilet paper, the Saran Wrap, and leftover Special K cereal, Sheriff Lamar Jenkins drove up with the keys. It made him sick to see all the things they had taken. Their cars and trucks were packed to the brim with anything they could get their hands on. They'd even taken her water hose and gardening supplies, and someone had even dug up all her gardenia bushes and had them in the back of their truck ready to go. The whole place had been picked clean.

The next week, all around town, it was so spooky to see the women wearing Darla's dresses, her shoes, and her blue wool coat. Lucille was sporting Darla's diamond ring and her gold bracelet, and whenever anyone looked at her funny she would glare at them and say, "She gave me these!" Later, sometime in the middle of the night, even Darla's septic tank had been stolen, driven away, and stashed behind a barn.

Wade and Sissy, not wanting to take any chances, claimed to find an old letter from Darla, which they had forged, stating that she wanted them to inherit her house if anything should happen to her. They showed it to a lawyer, who said they'd have to wait until the lab results came in and she was declared officially dead before they could proceed. Fingers crossed, it wouldn't be too long.

However, at present, there were only two people in the world who'd know exactly what the lab results would show. One was Darla herself, the other was her best and most trusted friend from teachers' college, Mrs. Myrtle Grooms, who lived outside of Jonesboro.

It had all started the morning Darla dropped her hand mirror on the bathroom floor and leaned over to pick it up. When she bent over and saw her face from that angle and noted how it had fallen over the years, it had scared her half to death. Good God, she thought, how did I get so old? I need a facelift, and I need it now. After her husband had died, she'd had her eye on Sheriff Lamar Jenkins, who was also a widower. She was never going to get him to propose to this old face. She found the number of a "LOW PRICE, EXCELLENT RESULTS" plastic-surgery clinic in Mexico. She called and made an appointment for the following month and was very pleased. They offered a special that they were running that month, including a tummy tuck and breast augmentation, all at half price, so she jumped at it. She was thrilled to be going, but she had to keep it quiet. Pot Luck was a hotbed of gossip, especially about her. Darla couldn't trust anyone in Pot Luck to keep their mouth shut, but someone should know where she was, in case something went wrong. So she called her friend Myrtle.

When Myrtle picked up the phone, Darla said, "I have to swear you to secrecy. I want you to take a blood oath you will never tell anyone what I'm about to do, and I'm only telling you in case something happens to me. Can I trust you, Myrtle?"

"What, are you going to murder someone?" asked Myrtle.

"No, but I am going to Mexico and getting my face done and a tummy tuck and breast job. And it's nobody's business. You know the Wombles. If they knew, it would spread through Pot Luck like wildfire, so I plan on just leaving town and not saying a word to anyone. Now, word of honor, if something does go wrong, I want you to tell people it was a heart attack, okay? I do not want to be a laughingstock with people joking about me dying getting plastic surgery. Okay?"

"Okay, but . . . where would I say you were?"

"You can say I had to run down to Mexico to take care of a friend. That's what I'm going to say if I have to, when it's over."

"Okay, but what about your gardenias? Shouldn't I run down and water them for you while you're gone?"

"I thought about that, but it would be too chancy. If someone saw you, they might start asking questions."

"But the gardenias might die in this heat."

"I know, but if it rains, they might make it till I get home. I won't be gone long, no more than three weeks. Here is my number at the clinic if you need me, but please, under no circumstances can you give it to anyone. Promise?"

"You know me, Darla, mum's the word. Good luck."

A couple weeks later, after getting a call from one of Darla's relatives, a frantic Myrtle had called the clinic in Mexico. "Oh my God, Darla, you have got to come home right now. I just got word that everybody in Pot Luck thinks you're dead!"

"What?"

"They all think you're dead."

"You didn't tell them where I was, did you?"

"No, of course not, but you have to come home right now. I think they're even planning a memorial service."

"Oh Lord. Well, I can't come home now. The recovery is taking longer than they thought and my face is all puffed up like a poisoned dog. If I come home now, they will all know exactly what I had done."

"Well, at least call them and let them know you're not dead."

"I will, but I can't do it just yet. Oh dear, I hate that this has happened. But maybe it will make them appreciate me more when I do come home. Don't worry, as soon as I'm better and my new face goes down, I'll call Lamar and let him know I'm alive and headed home."

Myrtle hated to be caught in the middle of such a big mess. But she'd promised not to spill the beans about Darla's whereabouts.

As for Darla, she felt bad that Lamar was thinking she was dead. But she was on a mission. And she'd come this far, so if she could hang on just a little longer, she could come home and snap up Lamar before some other woman did, so it was worth it!

Exactly three weeks later, after putting ice on her face day and night trying to speed things along, Darla looked at herself in the mirror at the clinic and thought, Okay, a little makeup here and there, and I'm good to go.

Lamar had been sound asleep when the next morning his phone rang. "Hey, Lamar, it's Darla."

"Darla." He sat straight up in bed. "Good God . . . are you all right?"

"I'm fine, Lamar, fine. Sorry I haven't called for a while, but I've been down here in Mexico helping out an old friend. I'm flying home tomorrow. Did you miss me when I was gone?"

"Miss you, oh my God, Darla. I thought you were dead. And so did everybody else. Do you have any idea what-all I . . . we've been through here?"

After Lamar told her what had happened at her house, so she wouldn't be surprised, and how her one niece Alice had been the only one who hadn't grabbed some of her things, Darla was furious. "Well, well. I sure am glad to know this, Lamar. I suspected they were just after my things, and now I know it for a fact!"

Lamar's first call was to Wade, and he was happy to make it. "Hey Wade, I've got really good news about Darla."

"Was it her ashes?"

"No, Wade. It turns out that Darla's not dead after all. She's just been out of town visiting a friend in Mexico. But she'll be home tomorrow. But I hafta warn you, Wade, when she found out what happened to all her things, she sounded mad as hell. No telling what she might do."

Upon hearing the news that Darla was not dead and would be home the next day, Sissy started running around the room like a chicken with its head cut off. "Oh

Jesus, oh Jesus, you've got to get everything back over there, or we're all gonna wind up in jail. Get the damn microwave and I'll get the toaster oven. Hurry!"

Within an hour after receiving the email, Darla's house was a beehive of activity, people running in and out, up and down the steps with dishes, clothes, bedsheets, furniture being put back in place, even though Darla's couch and chairs had been reupholstered in a bright red vinyl. Jay Jr. had either taken or sold all the pills he had stolen, so he didn't think he would be caught, but he did bring Darla's electric toothbrush back. Her other nephew Darryl was already across the country in her Mustang. There was no way he could get it back there in time. The gardenia bushes Alma had stolen had all died. Alma replanted them anyway, but couldn't water them because the hose was still missing. The only person who was glad to hear her aunt Darla was still alive was Alice, who cried when she heard the news. Her aunt Darla had sent her through teachers' college.

Yes, they were her relatives, but in many cases, as Darla found out, blood was not thicker than money.

So now she was able to make out her new will, leaving it all to her niece Alice, the only one who really cared about her. The rest had grabbed at chicken feed when they might have had caviar. And Darla was done with the whole lot of them. Good riddance.

When the forensic lab report finally arrived, it showed that the burnt remains found were those of Darla's beloved yellow lab, Buster, who had died recently at the age of fourteen, and whom she'd had cremated.

And as for Lamar Jenkins, although the whole affair had been upsetting to him, he was more than happy that Darla finally understood the whole truth about her no-account family. And with good reason.

This Valentine's Day, he had planned to ask Darla to marry him. And now he would not have to put up with all of her deadbeat relatives hanging around. After they were married, he was hoping to honeymoon in Mexico. He figured that Mexico must be a very restful place, because when Darla had come back home she sure looked rested. Younger, even.

The Honey Bee Cafe

It wasn't a very big town, and if you wanted to know what was going on, you went to the cafe. It didn't seat but about thirty people, plus eight at the counter, but it did a steady business, with loyal, steady, long-term customers. The Honey Bee Cafe had been open since 1936, and by now there were more honeybee-themed knick-knacks on every shelf, nook, and cranny than you could possibly count. Peggy, who ran the cafe, had been collecting them for over thirty years now and continued to get more, whenever one of her customers traveled out of state. Dave Whitfield and his wife had just brought her a plastic honeybee in a hula skirt from their vacation in Hawaii.

Dave, a man in his sixties, along with his buddies, Wayne, Jeff, and Mark, were all part of the local men's group that met at the cafe every morning for breakfast.

Most had been going to the cafe since they were in high school, and back then, Peggy, a cute-looking eighteen-year-old girl with curly brown hair and dimples, had been there behind the counter to greet them, and she still was.

So many years later, after they had all become successful middle-aged men, Peggy would still greet them with the same, cheerful "Good morning, boys" as they headed over to the same table where they had sat for years. Not only did they sit at the same table, they usually ordered the same thing. Coffee, bacon, fried eggs over-easy, and toast. Once, because of his cholesterol, Jeff had ordered the oatmeal, but just once.

For the guys, the cafe had become their home away from home. Along with the good food, and good friends, there was always fun to be had with Peggy. They loved to tease her and were always trying to make her laugh. And even though she pretended she didn't, Peggy loved it, and would kid right back with them. She'd say things like "Don't tell me men don't gossip. You boys are worse than a bunch of old ladies." Or "I don't know how your wives put up with you . . . acting like twelve-year-olds."

They also had their little rituals. Peggy knew the date of all their birthdays, and on their special day, each "birthday boy" got a big piece of cake with his breakfast.

So the morning Dave found out through his wife, who was in real estate, that unbeknownst to anyone, Nate Miller, who owned the building, was just about to sell the cafe to an out-of-towner who wanted to turn the space into an art studio, he was alarmed. When Dave shared this confidential information with his three friends at the cafe, they all went quiet.

They couldn't imagine their life without the cafe. It had always been there. For all their lives, it seemed, Peggy had been there in her crisp pink-and-white uniform and big smile. For as long as anyone could remember, Peggy had only taken time off from work for a few weeks, when she was nineteen and had her baby.

So what about Peggy? What was she supposed to do? She was supporting herself and her ninety-three-year-old mother on her salary. And she was too proud to ever accept charity.

Later that afternoon, Dave, who had been designated to speak for the other three men, walked up the narrow set of wooden stairs to Miller's law office above the dentist's office, and knocked on the door.

Dave sat across from Mr. Miller and said, "I hear you're thinking of selling the cafe?"

The old man was a little annoyed that Dave knew his business and said, "Not thinking about it, Dave, I am selling. Why?"

"Well, Nate, I want you to think again."

"What do you mean?"

"I mean, what is gonna happen is that you are going to call your buyer and tell him you just got a much better offer. And then you're going to sell it to me and the boys."

"Do you know how much he offered me?"

Dave smiled. "Don't matter, Nate. Whatever it is, we are prepared to top it. With one condition."

"What's that?"

"You sign a nondisclosure agreement, assuring us that you will never tell anyone, especially Peggy, that you sold the cafe. You just keep her on salary that we will pay. I want you to give her a raise, and tell her it was your idea, okay?"

Mr. Miller jumped at it, and even though Dave knew the old man padded the price he'd been offered, by that evening, the deal was done.

The next morning when they walked in the door ready for breakfast as usual, they heard "Good morning, boys," and all was right with the world.

Two Different Worlds

Velma and Cathy

The old lady stood on her back porch laughing at her two chickens, Harry and Bess Truman, who were running around the yard stirring up a fuss. And as usual, it just tickled her to death. She threw them another handful of chicken feed and went back in the kitchen.

Velma Ruth Vanderhoff, a sweet-looking apple dumpling of a lady, with snow-white hair as soft as cotton candy, was one of those rare creatures who had never left the place where she was born. Rarer still, she was perfectly happy living in the same little white wooden farmhouse on Route 8, ten miles outside Cottonwood, Kansas, where she had lived for the past eighty-three years. She was especially happy this morning. Velma had not seen her granddaughter Cathy for quite a while now, but she always received a long-distance phone call from her on the first of every month. And at exactly ten o'clock Central time, eight A.M. Pacific time, the phone rang. Velma picked up on the first ring with a great big "Well, hey there, honey! How are you doing way out there in California?"

Cathy Harris, an attractive forty-eight-year-old who wore her streaked blond hair pulled back in a ponytail, answered, "Just fine, Nana, how are you?"

"Still alive and kicking, but miss seeing your pretty face. I'm so disappointed you all couldn't come see me this year."

"I was sorry, too, Nana, but with David changing jobs and our moving and all, it just didn't work out."

"Well, hopefully you can come next year. It's been way too long."

"I agree. Oh, by the way, Nana, before I forget, did you ever ask them if you could get cellphone service yet?"

"Oh, yes. I asked, but I'm too far out, so all I have is just my regular old phone."

"Oh, too bad. Hardly anybody talks on a landline phone anymore. They text."

"Do what?"

"Text . . . send written messages?"

"On your telephone?"

"Yes, you just type in a message and send it and presto."

"Well, I never heard you could type on a phone."

"Oh yeah, and if you had a cellphone we could do FaceTime and I could text you photos instead of having to mail them."

"Oh, but Cathy, I look so forward to getting my mail from you. People don't write letters like they used to. All I get now are catalogs and the AARP magazine. Why, last week I even got an ad from the Neptune Society offering me a bargain on a cheap cremation." Velma laughed. "I tell you, Cathy, ever since I hit the big eighty, I'm on the old-lady mailing list for sure."

"Oh, Nana, don't say that. You're not an old lady."

"Yes, I am, but I don't mind. I aways liked older people, and now that I am one, I like myself even more. Everybody at church tells me I'm an oldie but a goodie."

Cathy paused for a moment then said, "I'm not sure if calling someone 'an oldie' is very appropriate. It sounds a little like ageism to me."

"Oh no, honey, they mean it in a nice way."

"Well, I don't want anyone hurting your feelings."

"They didn't. We call each other funny names all the time. And Cathy, I know you want me to get one of those new-fangley phones so you can type me things, but really, honey, I can't tell how you're doing if I can't hear your voice. Oh. Hold on a minute."

Cathy suddenly heard the phone clank down on something hard and her grandmother calling out in a loud voice, "Willard! Get out of here! Out, mister! Right now!" After a moment Velma came back on the phone. "Sorry, Cathy, now, where were we?"

"Nana, who's Willard? Are you all right?"

"Oh, Willard's just one of my silly blue jays. If I don't feed them on time, they just march on in the kitchen and fuss at me."

"Oh God, Nana, you don't let birds inside your house, do you?"

"Well, I don't let them, honey, they just decide to come in and let me know they're waiting for their breakfast. Now, where were we again? Oh, I know, tell me about my precious great-granddaughter, Tracie Ann. Is she still doing great?"

"Oh yes, and she said to say hello, and to send you her love. It's hard to believe she's going to be a freshman in high school this year."

"I know it. She was such a little thing the last time I saw her. I can't wait to see her again. And you tell that girl when I do, I'm just gonna squeeze her to death. I showed everybody at church the last picture you sent me, and everybody said she was looking more and more like a Vanderhoff every day. Isn't that great?"

"I guess so," said Cathy. "I never really thought about it."

After a moment Velma said, "What's wrong, honey? You don't sound very happy."

"No, I'm fine."

"Well, you don't sound fine. Are you feeling all right? Is anybody sick and you're not telling me?"

"No, everybody's fine, Nana. It's just that . . . well, I guess it's just that I'm worried about what's happening in the world. And I'm terribly concerned about climate change, aren't you?"

Velma thought for a moment, then said, "No, honey, not really. I kinda enjoy it, myself. Of course, spring is my favorite, but now fall can be awfully lovely too."

Cathy sighed. "No, Nana, I'm talking about global warming. My Save the Planet group is marching on Washington next month in protest. We have got to stop it, Nana. They say in order for our planet to survive, we should ban all gas-driven vehicles by the year 2035 or it's going to be too late."

Velma was surprised. "By 2035? Oh dear . . . that's not too far off, is it? Well, Cathy, I guess I'm doing my part and didn't even know it. Did I tell you I'm not driving anymore?"

"No, you didn't. Why not?"

"Well, about a month ago, when I drove up to town I put my truck in the wrong gear and backed myself up in a ditch. Took two tractors and a mule to get me out."

"Oh God, Nana. Were you hurt?"

"No, but it was the second time I'd done it, so my friends decided I didn't need to be driving anymore." She laughed. "Earlene said that me being out on the road was too dangerous for man or beast!"

"Nana, that's terrible, how are you going to get around?"

"Oh that's no problem, Ollie Nubbins and her husband, Verne, come out and take me up to town once a week to get my groceries, and Earlene and Felton pick me up every Sunday for church."

"But don't you hate having to get rides everywhere?"

"No, I look forward to it. And afterwards we always go over to the community hall for lunch and have a good time. Oh, and Cathy, guess what? This afternoon we've got a big cornhole competition going on in town and Bud is gonna pick me up and take me." Then Velma suddenly cried out, "Oh my heavens, just look at that. Can you believe it? The very day you call and my little yellow butterflies have just shown up. Hold on a second."

Cathy heard the same loud clack again, and her grandmother calling out in the distance. "Hello, you pretty little things, welcome back. I'm on the phone with my granddaughter Cathy in California. She says hey." Velma picked up the phone again. "My butterflies say hey back. Well, spring has officially sprung!"

Cathy shook her head in disbelief. Her grandmother never ceased to amaze her. How anybody could get so excited over a bunch of butterflies was beyond her. "Nana, how do you manage to stay so cheerful all the time?"

Velma laughed. "Well, all I know is I wake up, make my coffee, glad to have one more day. Because you never know, honey, life can change on a dime."

"Yes, but Nana, aren't you bored living out in the country all by yourself?"

Velma thought for a moment. "No . . . I don't think so, why?"

"Well, I know I would be, with nothing to look at but my own backyard."

"Oh, but Cathy, there're lots of things to see out there."

"What things? I mean, how long can you look at a chicken?"

"Loads of other things. I've got lots of rabbits, and chipmunks."

"I know, but Nana, you're still looking at the same old yard every day."

"But honey, like I said, it's never the same. It changes all the time. Spring is so pretty with my tulips and blue-bell vines all blooming, and last winter, the entire yard was covered with snow. Why, I could have been looking out at a Christmas card."

"Yes, but what do you do for mental stimulation? Do you still read, I hope?"

"I sure do, and I have my TV to watch at night. I get a lot of good programs. I like to look at all the old shows, like *Carol Burnett* and *The Waltons* and anything with Dolly Parton. I love her. And I look at the Game Show Net-work, that's always fun. But oh, Cathy, you should see my yard after a rain. Everything just sparkles. We had a big rain just last week, and guess what?"

"I have no idea," said Cathy, looking at her watch.

"After it was over, there was a big rainbow right over the henhouse. You can always count on old Mother Nature to put on a different show every day. And it's all for free too. That's why you and David and Tracie Ann need to move here. I never understood why people want to clump all together in a big city. We've got lots of wide-open space and fresh air, so come on here with me. Why, just think, Cathy, if you were here today, we could all go up to the cornhole tournament together, wouldn't that be fun? And there's a potluck at the church on Sunday, so you're missing a lot of fun events, with lots of good food."

"I'm sure, but Nana, David and I both have jobs here. And don't forget Tracie Ann has school."

"Oh, I know, just wishful thinking on my part. It's just I would hate to think that after three generations, this place will go to strangers, and your granddaddy wanted so much for you to have it."

Cathy looked at her watch again and sighed. She knew what was coming next.

"When your mother ran off and jumped on that Greyhound bus headed to Hollywood, oh, it liked to have killed us. Your poor granddaddy even drove all the way out there and tried his best to bring Ruthie Ann home, but she wouldn't listen." Velma shook her head. "After she won that Miss Sunflower Contest, she was convinced she was going to be the next Ginger Rogers or Debbie

Reynolds, and look what happened. She wound up a cocktail waitress and drinking her poor self to death."

Cathy sighed. "I know, Nana . . . I know."

"But thank heavens she left us you, sweetheart. I'll never forget the first time Ruthie Ann brought you home. Oh Cathy, you were the cutest thing! Do you remember how your granddaddy spoiled you? Carrying you around town on his shoulders, showing you off? You were so little, and we used to put you down for your nap on the glider swing on the porch. Do you remember?"

"All I remember is the chickens pecking my toes."

Velma laughed. "Your mother had you wearing that pair of little sandals, and the chickens thought your little toes were pieces of corn." Velma was silent for a moment. Then she said, "Oh honey, I miss you so much. So try and get here next year."

"I will, I promise. Listen, I have to run now, Nana, I've got a yoga class to teach, but we'll talk next month, okay?"

"Oh, okay, honey, but I sure loved our chat today."

"Me too."

"Be sure and tell everyone hello for me."

"I will. Bye now."

After Cathy hung up, she quickly reread the new ad for her yoga class that she'd just printed out on recycled paper, and was pleased with it. She quickly packed her bag, and as she headed out the door, she thought about the conversation with her grandmother. And yes, it was true her mother had been a sad case. But with all her mother's faults, she had at least gotten them to California and out of Kansas.

She was so grateful to be living in Berkeley, surrounded by educated, socially responsible people. And as much as she loved Nana, and would always be grateful to her for paying for her college education, it was getting harder and harder to communicate with her every month. She sometimes felt like she was talking to someone living on the other side of the moon. Cathy had grown up in and around Burbank, California, and had met her husband, David, when they were both students, while marching in a peace rally. She had never really known her own father. He had been only one in a series of not-so-nice men her mother had brought home, mostly drunks and would-be actors. So when she met David, a nice, clean-cut, socially conscious young man, it was such a welcome change. After David finished his graduate degree at UC Berkeley, they were married in a beautiful hilltop temple in San Francisco and settled in a small apartment near the Berkeley campus, where David taught, and very near her yoga studio.

Of course, before marriage, they had discussed the matter of having children, and both agreed that it felt irresponsible to bring a child into the world, particularly in these scary and uncertain times.

However, things don't always go as planned. Cathy was almost thirty-six when one morning, to her surprise, and despite using caution, she suddenly found herself pregnant. The news presented quite a dilemma, and had her and David wondering what they should do. However, the very next afternoon, a well-known San Francisco clairvoyant came to Cathy's yoga class and left a card that read: "Acceptance is honoring the universe, saying yes to the Divine Goddess within." Both she and David felt this was a profound message. Of course when Cathy told her grandmother that she was about to become a great-grandmother, Nana had been thrilled, and hoped if it was a girl they would name her Ruth Ann, Cathy's mother's name. But when the time came, she and David decided to name their little girl Tracie Ann, after a folk singer–activist they both admired.

A few minutes after their phone conversation as Cathy was riding her bicycle over to her class, she remembered something her grandmother had said and wondered, What is a cornhole? God, it sounded disgusting. She just hoped it wasn't dangerous and Nana wouldn't hurt herself. Cathy had tried for years to get Nana to move to California so she could keep a closer eye on her. But Nana wouldn't do it. She always said the same thing: "I can't leave my farm, honey, besides, I'm still hoping you'll come live here with me."

It was so sad. Cathy would never tell her grandmother

this, of course, but Cottonwood, Kansas, was the last place on Earth she could ever live. They didn't even have a Starbucks there.

Cathy stopped her bike at the corner and put one of her recycled-paper flyers on a telephone pole and rode on to the next pole.

ATTENTION

Please join us for a free one-hour introductory session
of
Quantum Mindfulness Meditation Yoga
with
Cathy Harris, Certified Yoga Instructor & Activist

Offering easy-to-utilize curated tools to foster a sense of empowerment and evolution toward self-realization.
A gentle gateway to guide you on your sacred journey to a state of nowness, to help you embrace your inner being and expand your worldview. A way-show-er and path connecting with the center of your universal and spiritual oneness. A space to examine the fluidity of one's inner search in a safe, inclusive, nonjudgmental environment, utilizing drums, chimes, crystals, and sound-bowl healing, in a smoke- and fragrance-free facility. Yoga mats provided. Vedanta Center, Suite 2
#Parking will not be validated

Meanwhile, back in Cottonwood, Kansas, Velma walked over and looked at the bright pink flyer she had taped to her kitchen cabinet.

HEY FOLKS

LOOKING FOR FUN AND EXCITEMENT?

Then come on down to THE PINK POODLE BOWL BAR
AND LOUNGE parking lot this Saturday at 3 for the
final cornhole playoffs!
It's now down to 2 teams.
This time it's the boys against the girls!
The Double-wides vs. the Amazon Queens
So come on down and root for your favorite team.
First prize will be a trip to the REGIONALS.
Runner up will receive FIVE FREE NIGHTS of bowling.
Third prize, free oil change and car wash at
Willy's Chevron. Hot Dogs and Beer, provided by
Hockum's Auto Supply.
Entertainment by Bill Eddie's band,
featuring Dave Bradford on steel guitar.
A night of line-dancing after the event.
Join us for an afternoon and night of fun and
free goodies!!!
Bring the kiddies. Babysitting provided.

Velma was really looking forward to going to the tournament. She was not very good at cornhole, but her friend Earlene was a whiz at it. Although Earlene was a thin, nervous little woman, she could flat-out pitch those bags into the hole every time. Too bad Cathy couldn't be here to see her in action.

Oh well, maybe next year.

Just then, Velma happened to glance out her kitchen window, and to her delight, saw that her yard was now filled with dozens more yellow butterflies, fluttering up and down and all around, and just like Velma, so happy it was spring again, so happy to be alive.

Don't Mess with Texas

Jo Ellen and Pauline

∼⟨⟩∼

Earle Pickett and his cousin Curtis sat parked outside the Dillard's department store in the Broadway Mall parking lot, waiting to make their move.

If all went well, it would be the third car they had highjacked in Texas this month. They had found from experience that the big shopping malls were easy pickings, and they now had it down to a science. Their main secret was the element of surprise.

They would arrive at the mall early, drive around the parking lot, pick out the car they wanted, and wait. When the owner came out and got in their car, Curtis would drive over close to it, and as soon as the owner put the key in the ignition and started the engine, Earle would jump out, run to the car, and force the owner out. Then he'd jump in and drive the car like hell all the way back over the Louisiana state line, with Curtis following close behind him. Then they would head directly to the used auto parts shop near Shreveport that they did business with and split the proceeds fifty-fifty. Earle had just turned twenty-three but he figured at this rate, he would be a millionaire by the time he was twenty-five. Who needed to finish high school?

Today they had their eye on that sweet-looking little red Trans Am parked all by itself with a TAMMY WYNETTE FOR PRESIDENT sticker on the back. Not only would it bring in a lot of cash, but they were banking on the owner being female. They only robbed women. It was so much easier, like shooting fish in a barrel. All you had to do was yell and flash a gun at them, and sometimes they got so scared that as an extra added bonus they'd leave their purse in the car. The last gal had eighty-eight bucks in cash, and a man's diamond ring in her purse.

Earle and Curtis had been in the lot since 9:30 that morning, watching the Trans Am and thinking whatever the owner was doing at the mall, they were taking a hell of a long time to do it. They were glad they had brought along those two bags of Doritos to tide them over, plus a couple of snorts of coke to keep them awake for the ride back to Louisiana.

It was late afternoon, around five, when two women came out of their shop, locked the door behind them, and walked toward the red Trans Am.

It had been a long day at work and they were happy to be headed over to the TGI Fridays to meet some friends for drinks. As they walked over to the car, they were still laughing at something that had happened at the shop that day, and Pauline, the larger of the two gals, clicked open the driver's side. Her friend and coworker, Jo Ellen, walked around to the other side and got in.

Damn! Now there were two women they had to deal with, but too late now. "Let's roll," Earle said.

As soon as Pauline had settled in, fastened her seatbelt, and put her key in the ignition, a skinny male figure dressed in all black suddenly appeared from out of nowhere, jerked open the door, and yelled, "Get out of the damn car, now!" He waved a gun in her face.

"What?"

"You heard me," he said, pulling on her arm. "Get out of the damn car, both of you. Get out now!"

Pauline was so scared, she couldn't move. Earle yelled at her again, "I SAID, GET OUT OF THE CAR NOW!!!!"

A frustrated Earle was struggling to undo Pauline's seatbelt and pull her out of the car at the same time, which was no easy task. Pauline was deadweight and still holding on to her steering wheel.

Meanwhile, as all the pulling and jerking was going on, Jo Ellen had ever so slowly and carefully slid her hand inside her big black bag and pulled out her weapon, then quickly reached across Pauline with it and said, "Freeze, you asshole. Don't move or I'll blow your damn brains out!" Earle suddenly saw the glint of the silver barrel and it was pointed at a spot directly between his eyes. Jo Ellen said, "Drop your gun. NOW!" Poor Pauline was caught in the middle of a standoff between two people with guns pointed at each other. "Oh Lord in heaven," she said.

But the standoff didn't last long. When Earle saw the steadiness of the woman's hand and the calm, steely look in her eyes, he had to make a decision. He quickly figured out that since her gun was real, and his was a fake, he'd better do what she said, or else have his head blown off. So he dropped his gun.

Jo Ellen got out of the car and said to Earle, "Now, turn around with your back to me, and don't move." Still aiming directly at his head, she walked over to the other side and kicked the gun he had just dropped out of his reach.

"Now, put your hands over your head . . . and don't move a muscle or I swear I'll fill your ass so full of lead."

"Okay, okay, lady," he said, and he put his hands up. Earle frantically looked to his cousin for help, but when Curtis saw that Earle was being held at gunpoint, and the way that woman was standing holding the gun with both hands, he figured she was most probably some kind of off-duty police officer. That's why he'd made Earle use a fake gun. But with Curtis's record, he couldn't take a chance on getting arrested for armed robbery again, so he took off.

Now Earle was left high and dry with this crazy woman and a gun pointed at his head. What was he gonna do? The only chance he had was to try to make a run for it. But Jo Ellen must have read his mind because she said, "And don't even think about running, because if you do, I promise you won't get far. Pauline, call 911 and tell them where we are."

Then she said to Earle, "Go on, buddy. Try it. I dare you. And if you ever wondered if there was life after death, you're about to find out. Now, get down on your knees and keep your hands over your head. NOW."

Earle could feel her gun poking him in the back of his head, so he did what she said. Then Jo Ellen said, "You little bastard. Trying to be a gangster, are you? Well, son, you just picked the wrong gal to rob. You little chicken-shit. Trying to steal some poor hardworking woman's car."

Pauline called out to her, "The police said they'd be here in just a minute."

When Earle heard the word "police," he started to turn around and look at Jo Ellen to see if he could possibly take her, but she said, "Don't do it," and once again, when he felt the barrel of her gun at the back of his head he changed his mind.

"Hey, Pauline," she said. "Come over here and look at this little skinny rat. What did you think you were doing, scaring my friend like that? You know what, Pauline? I don't think I can wait for the police to get here. I think I'll just go ahead and pop him right now. Get it over with."

"No, Jo Ellen, no. Wait for the police. You'll get in trouble if you do. Just wait. They'll be here soon. Let them handle it."

"Yeah, but I don't think I can wait." Earle felt the cold steel barrel push even harder. "Start saying your prayers, pal."

Pauline continued to plead with her. "Oh, come on, Jo, he's just a kid. Look at him. Don't shoot him. Remember what happened when you killed that last man?"

"Yeah, but he needed killing. And somebody had to do it."

Earle now knew he was in very big trouble and started moaning, "Oh, lady, listen to her . . . please don't kill me. Oh shit, oh shit, lady. I don't wanna die."

Jo Ellen said, "Sorry, son. I just can't help myself. I've got to do it; my fingers are jumping." Then Earle heard a loud click, and it scared him so badly, he peed all over himself.

Jo Ellen kicked him and said, "Now, tell her you're sorry for trying to steal a poor helpless woman's car."

"I'm sorry, I'm sorry."

"Put your hands back up . . . Say that you'll never do it again."

"I'll never do it again, I promise. Ohhhh shit."

Just then, they heard the siren and a police car pull up. Earle never dreamed he'd be so happy to see the cops show up in all his life.

Officer Ray Winn got out and walked over. "What's going on here, ladies?"

Jo Ellen said, "Officer, this punk here tried to steal my friend's car. There's the gun we got off of him. He's all yours."

As soon as Earle was being handcuffed by the other deputy and felt safe, he said to Winn, "Why are you arresting me? I ain't done nothing. That bitch just tried to kill me. She's the one you should be arresting. She's crazy. And she's got a gun."

Winn looked over at the attractive blond woman. "Is that true, miss?"

Jo Ellen looked surprised and said, "A gun? Me . . . No, I don't have a gun."

Pauline jumped in. "I saw the whole thing. She didn't have a gun, Officer. He's the one that had the gun."

Earle yelled, "She's lying, she's lying! She pointed it right at me. I heard her click the damn trigger. The bitch was gonna kill me, I tell you, she's got a gun!"

Officer Winn looked over at Jo Ellen again and suddenly noticed that there was something silver and shiny sticking out of her right sleeve.

He instantly placed his hand on his weapon in case she really was crazy and possibly dangerous. "What's that you have in your right hand, miss?"

Jo Ellen looked down at it. "Oh, this? Oh, this is just a curling iron." She pulled the rest of it out of her sleeve and snapped it a few times to show him how it worked, and then handed it to him. "I'm a hairdresser and I carry it in my bag with all my beauty supplies. That's our shop over there. The Curl Up & Dye Beauty Shop."

Officer Winn looked over and said, "Oh yeah, I've seen that place. But wait a minute, let me get this straight. You mean to tell me you kept this guy at bay with nothing but this curling-iron thing?"

"Well . . . I guess so. But it's not my fault that he thought it was a gun. I never said it was a gun."

Pauline said, "No, she never said it was a gun."

Earle was really frantic now. "I'm telling you, she had a gun. And she already killed another man too. Her friend said so, ask her."

The officer looked over at Pauline. "Did you say she had killed somebody? Is that true?"

Pauline shook her head. "No, Officer, she didn't kill anybody. I just made that up to scare him. We were just making sure he wouldn't run away before you got here."

"You say he had a gun?"

"Oh yeah," said Jo Ellen. "And he scared my friend here half to death sticking that thing in her face."

"Well, you took a mighty big chance," said Winn. "He might have killed you and your friend."

"No, not really. My boyfriend's an ex-Marine, and he taught me all about guns. I could see right away it was a fake."

The other officer, who had picked it up, nodded. "It's plastic."

Officer Winn stood there for a moment deciding what to do. This was a most unusual situation. A criminal apprehended by a curling iron. After a while he said, "Well, ladies, all I can say is, you make me proud to be a Texan."

He looked over at Jo Ellen and said, "But do me a favor. Don't be pulling any more curling irons on anybody, okay?"

"Yes sir, I promise."

Ten minutes later, Pauline and Jo Ellen were at TGI Fridays and had just ordered their first piña colada while Winn and his deputy were laughing their heads off as they drove over to the jailhouse with Earle Pickett in the backseat, yelling and cussing all the way.

A New Arrival

Oliver and Thomas

~⚬~

It was a wonder they hadn't given him a heart attack. A minute ago he had been sound asleep, all warm and cozy, minding his own business, when he was suddenly startled awake to the sound of strange people screaming at the top of their lungs. What in the world was happening? Then he felt himself starting to move. It was still pitch-dark and he couldn't see a thing. What in the heck was going on? Some man kept yelling, "Push! Push! Push!" and before he knew it, something or someone had grabbed him by the feet and jerked him up into this blinding bright light. Then, without any provocation on his part, a huge man wearing a mask and dressed in white brutally slapped him across the backside. Ow! You big bully! He wanted to take a swing at this guy, but before he could figure out how to do it, he was handed over to someone else and run across the room, thrown on some kind of hard surface, and was now being scrubbed all over with some kind of cold liquid that smelled just awful. Then he heard the man announce in a loud voice,

"Congratulations, Mrs. Speirs, you've got a healthy eight-pound, ten-ounce baby boy. Good job!"

Good job? Hey, wait a minute, why is she getting all the credit? What about me? And another thing. Nobody asked me about being born, I was quite happy where I was, thank you, and if this is any indication of being out in the world, I sure don't like what I've seen so far. These people are doing whatever they want with me, handing me around the room like a football or something and I can't do a darn thing about it.

And on top of that, he was freezing. Thankfully, he was now being wrapped in a blanket. They'd stuck some kind of hat on his head and placed him in his mother's arms. And now that he could get a good look at her, he thought, Hmmm . . . not bad. Nice eyes. But she does look tired. A few minutes later, he heard some heavy footsteps come rushing toward the bed and heard his mother say, "Oliver Henderson Speirs, say hello to your daddy."

Oliver? Good Lord, folks. I hate that name, thanks a lot. Then he got a good look at his daddy. Well, he doesn't show me much. This guy really needs a shave, and he doesn't look all that stable either. Too emotional for my taste. This may not go well, but we'll see. In the meantime he was hungry, but all they did was talk to him with all this gooey-goo stuff. Coochie-coo and stupid things like that. He endured it for a while, then he looked up at his mother, kicked his feet as hard as he could and said,

"That's enough of the baby stuff, I'm hungry now!" But evidently he wasn't forming words and all he could say was WHAAAA! But she finally got the hint, and soon he was busy nursing away, and glad to be so. What took you so long, is what I want to know.

Later, with his little tummy full, warm again, and snuggled up against his mother, he thought, This might not be so bad after all. Of course, later on he would have to do something about that name, but now he just wanted to sleep. He'd had a hard day, the hardest day of his life, was his guess.

But then, Oliver didn't know what was to come tomorrow. A little thing called circumcision. Ouch indeed!

What Oliver also did not know was that he had not been alone in his mother's womb, and he was not alone now lying in his little crib.

His specially assigned guardian angel, named Thomas, had been watching and hovering over him all the while. Thomas was a rather young angel, and it was a good thing. He could tell by the way Oliver kicked his feet and yelled that this boy had a lot of energy. And Thomas was absolutely right about Oliver.

As soon as little Oliver started walking, he was on the go from morning to night. Then it was run-run here, run-run there, climb up this, jump off of that, stick your hand in this . . . oh, it never ended. At the end of the day, Thomas was so happy when Oliver finally went to sleep at night, and he could get a little rest. But even then, he had to always keep one eye open, because Oliver would sometimes wake up and sneak downstairs to the kitchen and steal cookies. And when Oliver hit his teenage years it only got worse.

Why Oliver's parents would buy him a car was beyond Thomas. The way the kid drove scared him, but he got in the car with him. Part of the job.

However, it was never a pleasurable ride. Thomas spent the entire time saying, "Slow down! Watch out! Stop sign! Pay attention! Car coming around on your right! Look out!" If he hadn't been with Oliver, sending him those messages, the kid was so reckless, he would have killed himself, or somebody else for sure, before he was seventeen. Luckily Thomas was a member of the GAI union and did get a two-week vacation every year. And this year he really needed it.

Oliver had now started jumping off of a huge rock into a tiny water hole twenty feet below. The guy who filled in for Thomas while he was gone said to Thomas when he returned, "I feel for you, I don't know how you do it. This guy is shot out of a cannon. I'm exhausted."

Poor Thomas went back to work just in time to find out that Oliver had decided to take up hang-gliding. As if life wasn't dangerous enough he had to do this? Fly off the top of some mountain? Two weeks later, Thomas tried to warn him, but Oliver wouldn't listen, and bang. They hit the tree going at least thirty miles an hour, and it took the rescue crew fourteen hours to get there and get him down. And on top of that, Oliver had broken his leg. Thomas should have felt bad, but honestly he was relieved; maybe this would slow Oliver down a little, make him a little more cautious. But no such luck. While he was in the hospital, Thomas started looking at ads online for used motorcycles.

Oh no. He didn't know how much longer he could keep this guy safe, but he would keep trying. Next time he hoped he would be assigned to some sweet little girl, one who was careful and liked to just sit and color in her coloring book, and have people read her stories and would mind her parents. No more boys, please!

Thomas had hoped that when Oliver grew up he might slow down, but it was not to be. After graduating from Wharton Business School, he dove headfirst into every new and innovative venture he could. Thomas was busy night and day, carefully guiding Oliver through a mine-field of risky business start-ups that could have destroyed Oliver's chances for success. He had saved him from two potentially disastrous marriages and steered him to the right place at the right time to meet the perfect girl.

And Oliver never took a break, until the day came when he finally hit the jackpot. This very morning, he was being interviewed on the floor of the New York Stock Exchange by a CNBC business reporter who, just as the red TV camera light blinked on, announced, "I'm standing up here at the podium of the New York Stock Exchange, where Oliver Speirs, founder and CEO of Speirs USA, is just about to ring the opening bell, and as you can hear, amid much fanfare." There was a large crowd on the huge Wall Street trading floor below, applauding loudly as the bell began to ring in the background. The reporter continued, "Oliver, you've had many detractors betting against your company's new breakthrough method of efficient and eco-friendly lithium mining."

Oliver, cool and calm and in his element, nodded. "That's right."

"And yet here you are, making your company's debut on the exchange, and the stock price is on track to double as public trading begins today. Nobody thought you could do it. All I can say is, you must have a guardian angel somewhere to have pulled this off."

Oliver laughed and said, "I'm beginning to wonder that myself."

Thomas didn't hear that last remark; he was too busy ringing the bell!

Don't Forget to Write

Helen

This is a tale that really needs to be told, but I am only telling you, okay? There is an important moral to this story, but first, you should know a little more about Helen.

Helen was a very pleasant-looking girl, not pretty but not unattractive. "Plain" might be the term some (not us) would use. Her best feature was her smile, and sweet, eager-to-please disposition. From an early age, and without any of the usual promptings, she'd always help her mother set the table, wash the dishes, and was happy to babysit her younger brothers and sisters. She was raised in a nice-enough house, in a neighborhood where her father was the pharmacist at the Rexall drugstore on the corner. Helen adored her father and was never happier than at the times when he would bring her to work with him.

She loved being in the back room, helping him mix the different compounds, counting out pills, and by age twelve, she was able to read prescriptions almost as well as her father. Was it any wonder her dream was to one day marry a doctor?

After high school, her grades were good enough to be accepted at Cornell Medical College, and she was hoping to study biochemistry. As it turned out, she was the only girl in her class that year, but it didn't bother her; she just remained focused on her studies. However, in her second year, her main focus was on a certain handsome (she thought) freshman named Marvin Ray McWilliams from Salt Lake City, Utah. And the rest is history.

After they married, and at the beginning of his sophomore year, Marvin was finding his field of internal medicine to be too hard, so he switched to dental school instead. However, as they were still young newlyweds, and both of them were in school, money was tight, so they made the joint decision that Helen should drop out of medical college, get a job, and help him get through school. Then, after he set up his dental practice, she could always go back and get her degree.

And Helen was happy to do it. Always a whiz at numbers, she was soon handling the books and ordering supplies for three of the local drugstores in Ithaca.

Of course (you guessed this already), she never went back and got her degree. And after Marvin graduated, she continued to work, only this time managing Marvin's new dental practice and raising their twin girls, Carrie and Geri.

. . .

Thirty years later, Helen had just read a quote from former first lady Patricia Nixon, who had wondered who she would have been, had she not been Mrs. Nixon. Helen had never thought about it before, but she asked herself who would she have been, if she hadn't been Mrs. Marvin McWilliams. And as hard as she tried, she couldn't imagine it.

Helen, at sixty-four, was still a kind and caring woman, with short, curly gray salt-and-pepper hair, perhaps a tad matronly (but pleasantly so) and with that same smile that announced, "I'm very eager to please." Helen's main job in life was to make her husband happy, and to manage the McWilliams Dental Clinic, which now employed over twenty-three people. After working all day at the clinic, she would always go home just a little early, to cook Marvin's dinner and have it ready for him. She needed to make sure her husband had a hot meal every night. A meat, two vegetables, and a starch with as little salt as possible. Marvin had high blood pressure, and she was closely monitoring his cholesterol. And when Marvin was sick with a cold or a flu, Helen slept on a pad on the floor by their bed, so as not to disturb him, but in case he should need anything during the night. Both of her daughters were modern, independent women and were embarrassed by her behavior. Just last week, Geri had called Carrie and said, "You won't believe this. The other day I dropped by, and she was ironing his damn underwear. Ironing his boxer shorts, for God's sake."

"Well, that's a new one."

"Yeah, and I said, 'Mother, I can't believe you are doing that,' and do you know what she said? She said, 'Well, your daddy has very sensitive skin.'"

"Oh, I may barf."

"I know. Double-barf."

They loved their father but hated the way he let their mother wait on him hand and foot. And whenever they confronted him about it, he just shrugged and said, "Your mother wants to do it. I can't stop her. Talk to her, not me."

They still loved him, but they also felt that he was somewhat of a jerk. (Just how much of a jerk he was, they were soon to find out.)

Dr. Marvin McWilliams, a sandy-haired, fairly nice-looking man, was only a year younger than his wife and also vain about his looks. And throughout the years, the older Helen began to look, the older it made him feel.

Then, after a little prostate-cancer scare, Marvin had become increasingly unhappy. He began worrying about how much he'd been missing in his life, going to the office day after day, with only a two-week vacation to their same time-share home in Hawaii every year. He became restless and bored and felt he needed a change, and (you knew this was coming) her name was Cassandra.

The tall, thin, twenty-eight-year-old (or so she said), twice-divorced redhead with extra-large breasts had recently been hired as the new dental assistant. She had come highly recommended and (unfortunately) had been hired.

Helen should have been a little wary of her from the beginning. As soon as Cassandra arrived, the men in the office fell all over her, and she obviously liked the attention. And, also right from the beginning, Cassandra had completely ignored all the other women in the office and looked right past Helen as though she was a piece of furniture. Cassandra had been on the rove, looking for a rich, older man to marry. So what if Marvin wasn't quite the man of her dreams? His bank account certainly was.

As for Marvin, being flattered to death, he shamelessly flirted with this young, pretty woman (men can be so stupid about breast implants) and he began to realize he was married to a woman he was no longer attracted to, and in a job he was tired of. A perfect recipe for what was to come. A few months later, Cassandra quit her job at the clinic and (so she said) moved to another town.

In retrospect, Helen should have known something was up a month later when they had called from the pharmacy to say that Dr. McWilliams's Viagra prescription was ready for pickup.

She should have asked him about it at the time, but (get this) she didn't want to embarrass him, because men are so sensitive about that sort of thing.

Anyhow, not long after that, Marvin started arriving home a little later every night, until that fateful night when he came home right on time and said, "Helen, I need to talk to you. Come in the living room and sit down."

He didn't couch it, he didn't lead up to it or let her down easy, he just said, "Helen, I want a divorce."

She laughed and said, "Don't be silly. What is it, honey?"

"Just what I said. I am asking you for a divorce."

She looked at him and realized he might not be kidding. "But why? What have I done?"

"It's not you, it's me. I didn't mean for it to happen, but I have fallen in love with another woman."

"What? Who?"

"You know her. Cassandra."

"From the office? But she quit over a month ago."

"I know, we thought it would be easier for you, considering . . . and like I said, I didn't mean for it to happen. It just did. Anyhow, Cassandra and I want you to know that you will get half of everything. We'd like for you to keep the house, and we'll take over the time share in Hawaii. Fair swap, I think, and then after the first of the year, after I sell the practice . . ."

"Sell the practice?"

"Yeah, I'd like to retire as soon as possible. We'd like to travel for a little bit, and then . . ."

The stark reality of what was being said began to hit her, and she almost couldn't breathe. He was already using the word "we" and was planning the future that she had planned, only without her.

. . .

After he left that night, Helen tried not to get herself too upset. She'd been through this sort of thing before with Marvin. When he had been in his forties, he'd gone through the usual male midlife crisis and bought himself a brand-new bright-red BMW convertible and a series of hair implants. But this was more serious. Helen knew that Marvin had made out a bucket list. He had told her so, but she had no idea that "Get a younger wife" had been on it.

Marvin moved out of their house and into Cassandra's little house across town (which he had paid for) while Helen continued to run the clinic. Helen had hoped against hope that this was just some little fling, and in time he would get over it, come back to his senses, and come back home. After all, Marvin had sold that red BMW convertible after a year. But Marvin seemed determined, and had set up a meeting with a lawyer to proceed with the divorce. Her daughters were furious with their father for doing this, and worried about their mother, who didn't seem to be able to face the truth. Carrie said, "If Daddy does marry that woman, I just hope it's not in a church, because when they ask if anybody has any objections, you know Mother is gonna stand up with a twenty-page list."

Helen admittedly had behaved rather badly at the lawyers' office. But seeing the two of them together, holding hands in the parking lot, had been too much for her to bear. Poor Helen had gone totally to pieces and become hysterical, crying and begging him not to go through with it, to leave Cassandra and come back home. Lois, a friend of Helen's from the office who had gone with her that day, had to take her home and give her a Valium to settle her down.

She said to Helen, "Honey, that woman has her nasty little hooks so far in him, he's never gonna get away, even if he wanted to. You have just got to come to terms with it."

"But she doesn't love him like I do."

"He'll find that out soon enough. Don't worry."

But she did worry. She was concerned about his health. When Helen finally realized he was not coming back, even though Cassandra had made it clear she didn't want Helen anywhere near her, she showed up at their house with a typed list of instructions for Cassandra.

"Be sure and check that his prescriptions have not expired, and order his refills in advance. Make sure he takes both of his blood-pressure medicines. Also, he must have his prostate checked every three months, and here is a list of his low-salt recipes. Note, he is allergic to onions, and should not have red meat more than once a week. And two vegetables with each meal, one being a green vegetable if possible."

And if that wasn't enough, she showed up a week later and delivered a stack of his ironed boxer shorts, which Cassandra proceeded to throw in the garbage can, and Marvin caught hell over it.

The next morning Marvin called Helen at work.

"Helen, you have got to stop calling me. And stop just showing up at the house at all hours. It's upsetting Cassandra. She's talking about getting a restraining order. You have got to realize I am not your concern anymore, and you have just got to stop this."

"But how? How do I just stop loving someone, stop caring about what happens to them? I need to know if you are all right. If you need anything. I don't trust that woman to take care of you."

Marvin shook his head. "I worry about you, Helen. I think you need to see a doctor."

"Why? Tell me what's wrong with loving and caring about the man you married."

"I'll tell you. When it's no longer love but some insane obsession. Do you know how hard this is for me? If Cassandra found out that I was even talking to you, she would have a fit! After that scene you pulled at the lawyers' office, I promised her I wouldn't have anything more to do with you. Now, for God's sake, Helen, please let me alone."

The next day her oldest daughter called. "Mother, I just got a call from Daddy. He's terribly worried about you . . . we all are. You're embarrassing him, yourself, and us. Daddy's very upset. He's trying to get on with his life, and you won't let him."

Funny how things change. Just a couple of months ago, *she* was the injured party, the one who had been left. But now everyone was suddenly concerned with how *he* felt. Marvin had excused his behavior by claiming that he couldn't help falling in love with another woman. It wasn't his fault.

Well . . . she couldn't help how she felt either.

Helen knew Marvin and Cassandra were going off on a three-month European cruise (the very one that she and Marvin had planned to take after they retired) in less than a week. And once they were gone, there would be no way to reach him, and it was killing her.

It wasn't fair. Why should she be miserable? She knew while the two of them were off having fun, she would be worried to death about him. She had to do something now before it was too late.

Helen had booked Marvin's doctor's appointment a few months earlier, so she knew exactly when his next appointment would be, and she also knew it was her last chance to see him before he left. That morning, she parked in the lot of the doctor's office and watched him get out of his car and go inside the building. She had an extra key to his car and while he was in the doctor's office, she went over and slipped into the backseat and waited. After his appointment, he got in the car and heard a familiar voice say, "Marvin, it's me. Don't turn around." And of course he turned around and saw Helen sitting in the backseat wearing sunglasses, with a hat pulled down over her face.

"Jesus . . . Helen, have you lost your damn mind, what are you doing?"

"How was your appointment? Is everything okay? How's your blood pressure?"

"It's fine."

"Your prostate?"

"Fine."

"Did you remember to get your flu shot?"

"Yes, I got the damn shot, Helen, Jesus . . . you have got to get help. Are you going to force me to get a restraining order?"

"No, no. I promise you. This is the very last time I will ever bother you. Just do this one last thing for me, and I swear, after this I will get help. But in the meantime, I just need to know if you are all right. I know you can't call me when you're gone, and I can't call you. So I've made it easy for you. I've already dated these cards and addressed the envelopes and put stamps on them. All I'm asking you to do is, every two weeks, just check the boxes and put one in the ship's mailbox. Cassandra will never know. And I won't be sick with worry. Please. For old time's sake."

She handed him six self-addressed envelopes, and then got out and scurried back to her car. Marvin sat there, wondering what in the world was the matter with her. Had she finally gone completely insane? He took a card out of one of the envelopes and saw what she had written:

MARVIN-

CHECK BOXES BELOW:

☐ I REMEMBERED TO TAKE MY BENAZAPRIL
& DILTIAZEM
☐ I AM NOT EATING TOO MUCH SALT
☐ I HAVE CHECKED MY BLOOD PRESSURE TODAY

Marvin looked up in time to see Helen backing out of the parking lot, but not before she looked at him and mouthed the word *Please,* and drove off.

Good Lord. He sat there wondering what he should do with the envelopes. If he should just tear them up, throw them away, and be done with it . . . or what?

But it was such a small thing she was asking. He knew Helen, and she did not lie. If she promised him it would be the last time she would ever bother him, she meant it. And he had been married to the woman for forty years. But on the other hand, if Cassandra ever found out, there would be bloody hell to pay. He had discovered (too late) that Cassandra had a temper like he had certainly never witnessed. And whenever she lost it, she would fly into such a rage, he sometimes wondered if she wasn't trying to kill him. Just last week she had thrown a can of creamed corn right at his head and almost hit him.

He guessed he could take a chance and hide the letters among his underwear. He had to pack his own clothes now, so there was very little chance that Cassandra would ever find them. And it was the least he could do for Helen. She had done so many things for him in the past. Things he had never even noticed until he didn't have them done for him anymore. He found out (too late) that Cassandra didn't cook, or do laundry, or clean house. It seemed her favorite answer to any request he had was "Do it yourself. I'm not your maid."

The truth was that Helen and Marvin were now sort of in the same boat. If her daughters found out that she had even contacted him at all, they would probably never speak to her again. They were already mad and disgusted with her as it was. So it was imperative that they never find out, but still she really needed to get those notes from him. And a couple of times a month was all she needed for peace of mind.

Marvin and Cassandra left on the cruise, and the first two months Helen had been so relieved that he had mailed the envelopes and, on all four notes, he had checked all three boxes. But after the last month, the first envelope was a little late in arriving and when the last of the six envelopes arrived, Marvin had somehow forgotten to check the boxes. But he had remembered to send it, at least. But still it was a little worrisome.

Three and a half months went by, and Marvin and Cassandra were scheduled to have arrived home about two weeks earlier. Helen started driving by their house, and as far as she could tell, they had not come home yet, and she wondered why.

Finally one day, one of her daughters called and said, "Mother, we had not wanted to tell you, but Carrie and I are in Rome."

"Rome, Italy?"

"Yes."

"Why?"

"Well, a couple of weeks ago, Daddy started getting very sick, and they couldn't find out what was wrong. So the ship's doctor had him helicoptered off the boat and put into a hospital here, for tests . . ."

"Oh no! Is he all right? Does he need me to do anything? Should I come there? Oh my God. How is he?"

"Mother . . . that's why I'm calling. He didn't make it."

"What?"

"Daddy passed away a few hours ago. We're both so sorry to have to call and tell you this, Mother. Carrie sends you her love and we'll call you later. We're not sure what Cassandra wants to do about getting him home yet, but I'll be in touch, okay? Love you, Mother."

Helen hung up the phone and smiled. Well, well, well. Right on schedule. She had timed it just perfectly. She had first come up with the idea while reading one of her favorite English mysteries, *Murder in a Little Pudding*. And using her knowledge of chemicals, and how to mix them, it would be easy to do. Her plan had obviously worked beautifully. She had added the exact correct tincture of arsenic with various other toxins to the glue on the flaps of the envelopes that Marvin had to lick to seal. One every two weeks. Just the right amount to slowly build up in his system and finally take him out for good three months later.

There would be an autopsy, of course, and they would be sure to discover that Marvin had been poisoned, but Helen was not in the least bit worried. Although she may have looked rather sweet, she was also smart as a whip. Much smarter than her husband had ever been. Helen knew from her mystery books that they always look for the murder weapon first. But in this case, the murder weapon had been mailed right back to her, and as soon as they arrived, she had quickly disposed of each note and its envelope. And of course, even if she did have a motive, she was nowhere near her husband at the time of his death.

How could she possibly have had anything to do with it?

Besides, the current wife, who had been the only one with him day after day at the time of his death, would be the main suspect.

And anyone with eyes to see would know that this younger woman had only married the man for his money. So the police might search Marvin and Cassandra's house for clues. And when they did, they might even find a small bottle with traces of arsenic stashed in a drawer in their garage. Helen should know, because she was the one who had put it there. And Cassandra (hee-hee) would have a hard time explaining that to the police. No, things were not looking good for dear old Cassandra.

Helen reached over and picked up the *Co-Dependent No More* book her daughters had given her and threw it in the trash can. She wouldn't be needing that anymore. And yes, she had taken rather extreme measures to achieve the goal. But really. The very idea. After devoting her entire life to this man, working like a dog to please him, day and night for the past forty years, this Cassandra thought she was going to waltz in the door and wind up with half of everything they owned, everything she had worked for? The clinic? The vacation house in Hawaii? And her husband too? I don't think so!

Helen had already written Marvin's obituary, and it was ready to go, so there was really not much else to do now but wait.

So she decided she would get dressed and take herself out for a wonderful dinner somewhere really special.

So the moral of this story is:

Be nice to the ex-wife, or you may live to regret it.

Cassandra certainly did. Two months later, she wound up in the slammer for something she didn't do. But not to worry, she still has her implants and a few good years left. If she gets parole anytime soon, that is.

The Science Project

Edwin

Monica came into her twelve-year-old son's room and said, "Come on, honey, put that away now, your dinner's on the table."

"Okay, Mom, be right there in just a second," he said. "I'm almost finished."

"When is your project due?"

"Tomorrow."

"Well, good. I'll be glad. This room is just a mess."

Monica walked back into the dining room and her husband said, "Is he coming?"

She sighed. "He said he'd be here in a minute, but you know what that means, so let's just start. No point in everybody's dinner getting cold."

"Is he still working on that same science project?"

"Yes, and you know Edwin. He wants it to be perfect."

"He's been in that room for over a week. What is he working on?"

"I don't know, he tried to explain it to me. He said he was working with atoms—helium and I think he said hydrogen? He's trying to set up some sort of time-controlled explosion, and find out if it causes lots of round matter to form? I don't understand it all."

Thirty minutes later, Edwin ran into the dining room all flushed and quickly sat down. "Sorry, sorry, but I had to finish adding my own live DNA components."

His father said, "What is it you're trying to do, son?"

"Well, if I can compress all the particles with the right amount of heat, I could get an explosion big enough to set it all in motion. I'm trying to create new galaxies of planets and then watch and see if anything evolves. Like a new species of intelligent life or something."

The next afternoon, Mr. Allen, Edwin's science teacher, sat at his desk grading all the science projects. He hated to give Edwin a D. He could tell Edwin had put a lot of time and effort into the project. However, his theory would never work. Even if the explosion did ultimately create new planets with live DNA, it could never survive that far away from its source, much less evolve into anything close to intelligent life.

Mr. Allen took another sip of his coffee and weighed his decision.

He could give him a C minus, maybe. But on the other hand, Edwin was his best student, and he didn't want to discourage him. So he changed the grade to an A. The next day he advised Edwin to go ahead and try it if he wanted to, and see what happened.

. . .

Much to Mr. Allen's surprise, after Edwin had set his "Big Bang" project in motion, a number of different galaxies had formed. But what was even more amazing to Mr. Allen was that some of the live DNA did manage to survive and intelligent life began to form on one of the planets. He decided that Edwin was either lucky or a genius, but either way, he was glad now that he had given him that A.

And even today, each night before he goes to sleep, Edwin always checks in on Planet Earth with his microscope to see how his project is coming along. He's been disappointed so far. He'd hoped he would be able to communicate with them by now. Oh well. They have a long way to go, but he isn't giving up. Edwin is still dreaming about one day winning first prize at the science fair.

Seat of the Matter

Cathy and Velma

At around 11:20 A.M., the phone rang inside a small two-bedroom apartment and a voice machine answered.

"Hello, this is the Harris family residence, wishing you peace on this spiritual journey we call life. Please leave a message after the beep." Cathy Harris had just finished her daily journaling and was in the other room doing yoga. She was sitting quietly in the lotus position when she heard the message coming through.

The voice on the line said, "Cathy? I hope this is Cathy. Anyhow, this is Earlene Moats calling you from Cottonwood, Kansas, and I'm calling about your grandmother, Velma. I'm afraid there has been a little incident, and . . ."

Cathy quickly jumped up, ran into the other room, and grabbed the phone. "Hello!"

"Hello, this is Earlene Moats. I'm calling to . . ."

"Hello. Yes, this is Cathy. What's happened?"

There was a pause. "Is this the machine talking, or is it you?"

"It's me, it's Cathy. I'm here."

"Oh, well hey Cathy, how are you?"

"Fine, just fine."

"Good, now, I didn't want to worry you, but Velma's over at the hospital. She had to have a chair removed, but they checked her out and she seems to be doing okay."

"A what removed? What?"

"A chair. See, here's the thing. Early this morning, Velma said she carried one of those old canvas folding chairs out to her back garden to see if she could see any baby rabbits. This is the season for them, and she has tons of rabbits out there on her farm. Anyhow, she said that when she went to sit down, the whole dang bottom fell out of the chair, and she wound up with her behind flat on the ground and her legs sticking straight up in the air and she was stuck."

"What do you mean stuck?"

"Well, after she fell through the seat, she got stuck inside the chair frame and couldn't move. And it's just a good thing Felton went out there to bring her that bowl of macaroni and cheese I made, because he said as soon as he opened the gate, he could hear someone calling out, 'Help, help,' and he walked back there, and there she was, stuck in the chair frame with her legs sticking up in the air. So he runs over and tries to pull her out, but he couldn't get her out for love nor money, so he called the fire department and they came out and tried to pull her out, but the frame wouldn't come loose, so they picked her up, chair and all, and hauled her over to the hospital, where it was removed. She couldn't walk for a few hours, her legs had gone numb on her, but she's up and walking now. Poor thing was stuck out in that yard for over three hours, and if Felton hadn't just happened to go out to her farm today, she might have been out there all night, with nothing on but a thin little house-dress. It's a good thing we don't have coyotes here, or she could have been eaten alive, nothing left of her but bones. But she's fine now, and she'll probably call you later on as soon as she gets home. Felton's going to be driving her out home as soon as they release her."

Cathy thanked Earlene for the call and forgot about finishing her yoga stretches. She was still holding the phone waiting for Nana's call when her daughter, Tracie Ann, came in from school. She looked at her mother and could see something was up.

"What's the matter, Mom?"

"Oh, I just got a call. Nana's in the hospital."

"Oh no, what's wrong with Nana? Is she sick?"

"No, honey, it's just a minor procedure. She had to have a little something removed, but she's fine now." Cathy didn't want to say it was a chair. Tracie Ann adored her great-grandmother and it might upset her.

· · ·

A few hours later, when the phone rang, Cathy quickly picked it up.

It was Nana. "Well, I *wish* Earlene hadn't called you. I didn't want you to worry."

"Nana . . . are you hurt?"

"No, honey, a little embarrassed is all. Just about everybody in town has seen my britches. Have you told Tracie Ann what happened?"

"No, not the details."

"Good. I don't want her to know her great-grandmother doesn't have more sense than to try and sit in an old, rotten, falling-apart chair. Imagine. Having a chair stuck to your behind all day. But we did have a good laugh over it, I'll say that. After they got the chair off, everybody at the hospital applauded. Anyhow, I did want to warn you. Don't sit in any old canvas chairs, especially ones that are old and have been sitting out in the rain."

"Oh, Nana, I'm so sorry that happened to you. What am I going to do with you?"

Velma laughed. "Who knows what I'm going to do next? Just another reason you need to come see me this spring."

"I agree, Nana. Hopefully sometime after school is out. Maybe the end of May?"

"Oh goody. Now I'll have something wonderful to look forward to. And you tell my precious Tracie Ann that her nana can't wait to see her again.

"But now, Cathy, here's the best part. While I was out in the yard waiting for somebody to come find me, I saw some of the most precious baby bunnies you have ever seen just jumping around and playing."

"That's nice, but do you need anything, Nana? Do you have food?"

"Oh yes, I have a big bowl of macaroni and cheese from Earlene, and those cute little nurses sent me home with some donuts. But you know, Cathy, when I was out there waiting I think I changed my mind about something. I used to wish that if I ever came back as something else, I could be a bird. But today I got to thinking I'd like to be a bunny. They have more fun and they are so darling, with their little cotton tails. What would you want to be if you could come back as something else?"

"Oh, Nana, I don't know. I'm not even sure if I'd want to come back, the way the world's going."

"Well, I'll tell you what. After I'm gone, whenever you see a bunny, be sure and give it a carrot or something, because you never know: that bunny you see might be me."

"I'll remember that."

"Well, honey, I've got to go get in the tub. The doctor said to take a hot bath with Epsom salts, to relieve the soreness. They like to have never gotten that chair off me. They had to pull at me every which a-way. So like I said before, whatever you do, be careful where you sit."

· · ·

When her husband, David, came home from work, Cathy took him into their bedroom and told him what had happened. Upon hearing about the saga of the chair vs. Nana, he burst out laughing.

"It's not funny, David, she could have killed herself."

"I know, but she didn't. Oh, I would love to have seen those doctors' faces when she came through the door with that chair stuck on her backside." Then he burst out laughing again.

"I don't think it's a bit funny."

"Yes, it is, where's your sense of humor? It's hilarious."

Just then, Tracie Ann came into the room. "Hey, what are you two laughing about in here?"

Cathy gave David a look, but answered sweetly, "Nothing, honey. Your father is just acting silly, that's all."

Later that night, Cathy thought about David's reaction and was still a little upset with him. She failed to see the humor in an eighty-four-year-old woman being trapped in a chair, out in the middle of nowhere, with her legs sticking straight up in the air. She could still hear him giggling in the bathroom. Honestly, men laugh at the strangest things!

The Dreaded D Word

Marion

Mrs. Marion Thornton Smith was still reeling from the shock of unexpected bad news. She was sitting in the study on her great-grandmother's Victorian sofa that had been shipped from England in 1804, along with the rest of the extensive dowry befitting a young lady of her class. And of course Marion had kept all of the family things together. I mean, you just have to, don't you? You owe it to your ancestors to caretake their beloved valuables, for heaven's sake.

But what would she do now? She was a lady of a certain age and it had already happened to several of her other friends, but somehow you just never dream it could happen to you. And so soon. Marion had assumed she had a lot more time left. But evidently not.

Her money manager, Mr. Newton Trott, of Trott & Crumble Accounting had just called and informed her that due to low stock performances, drops in the markets, et cetera, she would soon be running out of money. That was when Newton had uttered the dreaded D word.

He said, "Marion, I am afraid you are going to have to downsize."

Well, he might as well have shot her through the heart with a bullet.

"But Newton, how can that be? I thought Herbert left me with plenty of money."

"Oh he did, Marion, but that was almost sixteen years ago, and with all your household and living expenses it's as though you're tearing up hundred-dollar bills every week. And soon enough . . . you will run out."

After her husband, Herbert, died, their accountants had paid all of her bills. She had no idea about the cost of household expenses or what her housekeepers, gardeners, pool maintenance people, and so on cost per month. She never even thought about it. And now Newton had just informed her that she was actually going to have to sell her house.

He had said, "Marion, you simply cannot afford to keep it anymore. The place is just a money pit. We need to sell it and put that money in the bank so you will have something left to live on. You don't want to outlive your money and wind up with nothing."

That statement had really alarmed her. A friend of hers had made the mistake of outliving her money, and she wound up in a low-income retirement home on the other side of town, with people she didn't even know.

Naturally, Marion had been aware that her house had needed a lot of work lately. She'd replaced her roof, two furnaces, and had the pool replastered, but she had no idea, nor had she really cared, how much it had all cost. She had assumed she was well-off and always would be.

Good Lord, now what?

Her large, sprawling redbrick English Tudor home with its two acres of gardens had been built in 1920, and sat atop a mountain in an exclusive neighborhood overlooking the city. At one time, everyone aspired to own one of these landmark homes. But as her neighbors recently found out, the new homebuyers who were moving to town didn't seem to want the big, older homes anymore with a separate kitchen and a formal dining room. They now wanted a large kitchen/family room, where they could all sit, look at TV, and eat at the same time.

Even worse, as soon as some of the other homes like hers had been sold, the new owners had knocked them down to the ground and replaced them with huge, ugly, tan, sprawling megamansions. Marion had been in a few of those new houses, and everything inside and out was the same color—a sea of bland beige and white. To her horror, some even had large movie posters hanging on the wall, passing as art. And there had been so many new people moving into the neighborhood that she still didn't know most of them. At this point there were only four of the original homes left standing. Hers, two at the end of the street, and her longtime neighbors Stan and Barbara's house next door.

It used to be such a friendly, close-knit neighborhood, but not so much anymore. The new people seemed to all be joggers who never waved or smiled as they ran by. But they were everywhere now.

In the past, when Marion went over to the country club, she had known everyone by name, from the staff down to the valet parking crew. Now she hardly recognized a soul. And in just the past five years, the dress code had totally gone out the window. She was appalled at what she saw coming into the dining room now. People wearing tattered jeans and young girls in what looked like short little baby-doll dresses and combat boots. Also, she was appalled at the new members' lack of manners. They never said thank you or even looked at the waitstaff. She had seen one man come in and just toss his coat and hat at Mrs. Porter, the receptionist, and keep walking. And the interior of the club had just been redecorated to appeal to the younger members.

Evidently, the younger members had no taste, and as Barbara had said, the club now looked more like the lobby of a Marriott hotel instead of the cozy, traditional club that it once had been.

True, that entire area of town was not the same anymore, but even so, it was the only area Marion had ever known. She had grown up in the house down the street. And even if what Newton said about her finances was true, where would she go? And more important, who would she be without her house? It was her pride and joy. For years, no matter who she had been introduced to, they had always said, "This is Marion, she and her husband own the big Thornton Smith home up on the mountain."

Not only that, she was used to living in a large, rambling home. Good Lord, she would be smothered half to death living inside some tiny condo or apartment without her beautiful view of the city. So no, absolutely not. Selling her home was definitely out of the question.

Marion picked up the phone and called her son, Preston, in Washington and asked his advice. Unfortunately he was not much help. He said, "Mom, I don't think you have a choice. Newton is right, you need to sell it sooner rather than later. We don't know where the market is going, so I say get it sold now while you still have a market left."

"But Preston, where will I go?"

"Oh, I'm sure you'll find someplace you like. Like that place where Aunt Kitty went. That was nice."

"Preston! Kitty was in memory care, for God's sake! I'm not going to some retirement home!"

"Well, like I've said before, you're always welcome to come here with us. Don't forget we have that nice little granny flat. We just put in a new little kitchen and it's already plumbed to install a walk-in tub. So it's right here waiting for you. Just say the word."

Marion hung up and thought to herself, Well that's not going to happen. She didn't know a soul in Washington. Besides, her daughter-in-law, a Yale-educated lawyer, was not one of her favorite people. She talked too fast and it made Marion nervous.

Now not only was Marion facing the humiliation of going broke, her entire world had just been pulled right out from under her in less than thirty minutes. She quickly looked at herself in the mirror to make sure she was still there, and to her relief, she saw a lovely, well-dressed, beautifully made-up, slightly older lady, wearing a colorful and charming scarf, looking back at her. Good heavens, what was Preston thinking?

Imagine, her own son had just used the term "granny flat"! She would just as soon have someone stick her in the eye with an ice pick!

Still a little dazed from it all, Marion got up and walked down the hall and sat in her living room. Give this up? She sat down on one of the floral chintz sofas and looked all around the large room. How could I ever give this up? This is not just a house, it's a living thing. It's me. And a lifetime of my memories.

She sighed as she glanced over at the beautiful harp sitting by the grand piano in the corner, and closed her eyes, recalling so many lovely evenings spent in this room. Why, she could almost hear Madeline playing the harp, and George on the piano and see the entire smoke-filled room, and hear the clinking of glasses, the laughter of happy, well-dressed people throughout the entire house and on out to the outside terrace.

She and Herbert had been patrons of the Birmingham Ballet, the museum of art, the symphony. At one time she had been president of the little community theatre and had even appeared in several plays.

So many special gatherings of friends had taken place in this very room. Cast parties, fundraisers, parties for visiting celebrities.

Everybody knew that the Thornton Smith house was always open for a good cause. Susie, the society columnist, had always referred to her as "Birmingham's Premiere Hostess." But those days were gone now.

Nobody entertained at home anymore, not like they used to. Even she only did five major events a year, when at one time there would have been at least twenty.

On all her coffee tables in the living room, the study, and the den were her large sterling-silver cigarette table lighters, along with the crystal ashtrays that she and Herbert had purchased in London. She remembered a time when the ashtrays had to be emptied three or four times in an evening, but hardly anyone smoked anymore. She had kept them on all the tables just in case. She never wanted a guest to feel uncomfortable.

She also had a large collection of English Staffordshire

porcelain dogs from her mother. In the dining room were all of their silver candelabras, and in the den, assorted silver-framed photos.

As she sat there in tears, she realized that for the past sixteen years she had been living in a state of denial. It had never even occurred to her that this day would come and she would be leaving her home forever. What would her poor house think, with total strangers suddenly moving in? Not just strangers but maybe even Yankees.

What a scary place to suddenly find oneself, she thought, when just this morning she had been so secure, so happy, looking forward to hostessing her garden-club luncheon out on the terrace this spring.

But now, if what Newton said was true, without her home and her things, she really had nothing to look forward to ever again.

Nothing but some bleak, unknown future, watching her world becoming smaller and smaller, until one day she would just disappear. She almost wished she hadn't lived long enough to see it happen.

Newton called back later that afternoon and said, "Now, Marion, I've just spoken with Preston, and I know you are not happy about this, so before we do anything, let's just have someone come in and give us an idea of what you can expect to get for the house and go from there. Let's just try and make this transition as easy as possible, okay? I know it's hard, but we'll all just have to face the reality of it."

Marion had never understood why people were always so keen on facing reality. She didn't care much for reality, she never had. She preferred her own reality, where everything was beautiful, everyone well-mannered and soft-spoken. She did not want to face the cold, hard, cruel facts of life. But the thing she had always avoided was now standing before her and staring her right in the face.

After a long night of heartbreak and tears, Marion realized she had only three choices left:

1. Kill herself
2. Kill Newton
3. Meet with the realtor

By morning Marion had decided to go with number 3. Find out how much the house would sell for. She would like to have enough money left over after taxes, commissions, and capital gains so she could give all her sweet, loyal workers a really nice bonus, including her hairdresser and Lulu, her darling nail lady, and give the rest to all her favorite local charities. Then after that, maybe she would kill herself.

Marie Larkin, the realtor who had handled several home sales on Marion's street, was right on time. She was pleasant enough, and walked through the entire house with Marion, looking around, asking questions and making notes. Afterward, they sat down in the living room and Marie told her what she thought. She said, "Considering recent comparable sales, and the acreage and square footage, I believe we can easily put the property on at two million five."

Marion was very pleased to hear that.

Then Marie said, ". . . about the house. I think in its present condition, I would not advise having an inspection done. It will take a lot of time and money to bring it up to code. So my advice is to just go with an 'As-is' sale. I think the view is going to be our main selling point anyway."

"I see."

"Great. So I'd like to begin showing it right after the Super Bowl. Can we do that, do you think?"

Before Marion had a chance to reply Marie continued, "But before we show it, we're going to need to stage it."

"Stage it?"

"Yes, we do it now with a lot of our properties. Clear out all the personal items, photos, excess decorations." Marie looked over in the corner and said, "We'll probably have to remove a lot of the larger pieces, like that harp thing over there, and the piano. Create more space. Our office has a great team that does all my staging. And I'd like to get them here in the morning, if that's all right."

Marion said, "But I don't understand. What's wrong with the way it is?"

Marie gave her a sweet little patronizing smile. "Well . . . and I don't mean this in an unkind way, but the house is a bit dated, and our high-end buyers now are all looking for something a little more spacious and open with less, well, clutter."

Marion was confused. "Clutter?"

"Yes. Too much stuff."

After the realtor left, Marion almost cried. Four generations of loving and caring for your lovely family things and this *Marie* person thinks it's clutter.

An hour later Newton called. "I just talked to Marie and she said she wants to put it on the market right after the Super Bowl."

"I know that's what she wants, but Newton, that's so soon. I need more time . . . I mean, what if it sells right away? Where will I go? I can't just pick up and leave. I'll wind up living on the streets."

"No, of course you won't. And I've thought about that. Another one of my clients, Katherine Rye? I think you know her."

"Oh yes, we had our coming-out parties the same year."

"Well, she's going on a world cruise with her daughter in mid-February and her guest unit at Highland Towers will be empty and she said she would consider subletting it."

Marion was alarmed. "Newton, you didn't tell Katherine Rye that I had to sell my home, did you?"

"No, I said I was looking for a friend, but I think we should go ahead and rent it. Just in case the house does sell fast, so you have a place to go. It's a really nice one-bedroom, with a nice kitchen."

Marion rolled her eyes. "Newton, I've been in Katherine's unit; it's no bigger than a matchbox. There's not enough room in there for all my clothes and makeup, much less me!"

"I understand it's not the space you're used to, but with rents being what they are, we might need to jump at it. Bird in the hand."

"But what about all my furniture? My rugs, my paintings. My things?"

"Well, Preston and I think you should take what little furniture you need and get rid of the rest. You're going to have to sooner or later, why not do it now, get it over with? In the meantime we can get you a little storage unit to put whatever it is you think you can't live without. But I'm hoping you won't keep anything that you don't need. I have clients who are spending thousands of dollars a year paying for storage bins full of stuff they are never going to use. I don't want that to happen to you. Best to make a clean break. I'm sorry about all this, Marion. But I know that's what Herbert would have advised too. And oh, is nine o'clock tomorrow okay? Marie wants to bring the stager in and get the ball rolling."

The next day, a tall blond person with a loud voice named Connie, and her assistant, a thin little woman named Dot, showed up and proceeded to shoot through Marion's entire house like a dose of salts. Upstairs, downstairs, in the attic, down to the basement, opening every drawer, every closet, every cabinet, with Dot trailing behind Connie making a list. Unfortunately, Marion had excellent hearing and could hear Connie whispering instructions as they entered each and every room. "All the rugs have to go, except in the dining room and living room. All the figurines and things off the shelves, except the books. The entire attic has to be cleaned out and all the closets. And we need to change out these old sofas and chairs. Let's lose the floral curtains and the paintings, all the Venetian blinds. I don't know what we can do about the study. It's as dark as a mole hole." As they swept past Marion through the breakfast room to the kitchen she heard, "God. Just leave it. It's a disaster. Just get rid of most of the dishes and all those damn teapots in the window. All the tea sets. We're gonna need a moving van to get all this crap out of here."

Later, when Connie announced they were finished, they sat down in the breakfast room and Connie said, "Sorry to take so long, and by the way, lovely view you have here."

"Why, thank you," said Marion, hoping to have a longer conversation, but Connie handed her a sheet of paper and continued.

"Here are the things we need for you to clear out as soon as possible. We'd like to start staging next week, if we could."

Marion looked at all the items listed and was stunned. It was almost everything she owned.

"But . . . where am I supposed to put all these things?"

"Well, you can always store them. Or sell them."

"But . . . how do I do that?"

"Oh, we work with a great company that can handle all of it for you. I'll leave a brochure on the table."

As the two women walked back to their car Connie said, "Wow . . . that was a trip back to the forties. I felt like I was walking inside some old movie."

"Yes," agreed Dot, "it was sorta like some old-timey museum."

"And did you catch all the ashtrays and the cigarette lighters still out on all the coffee tables? I expected to see Bette Davis walk in at any moment. And all those stupid dog statues everywhere. I feel sorry for her. She's got an awful lot of crap to get rid of."

As Marion sat going over the list of all the things she had to do in such a short time period, she was over-whelmed with anxiety.

1. Clear out her entire attic.

How could she? It was jam-packed to the rafters with Christmas decorations, old toys, books, paintings, sets of old golf clubs, tennis rackets, croquet sets, plus that big chest of drawers full of board games, and that was just what she could remember.

2. All her drawers and closets.

She went upstairs and opened the door to the large walk-in closet Herbert had built for her. She looked at the rows and rows of formal gowns, dresses, coats, jackets, shelves of handbags, shoes, hats, and her collection of Hermès scarves, most of which she hadn't worn in years. She even had her old wedding dress carefully wrapped and boxed on the top shelf. Where would she put all of her clothes?

Connie had also said she needed to clear everything off the sideboard in the dining room, and off all the tables in the entire house. Marion went back downstairs and looked at all the things she had to remove. Almost all of her furniture had to go. But where? Preston and his wife made it clear they didn't want anything. For some Godforsaken reason, they liked midcentury modern. So there was no need to save anything for them. But how could she pick and choose what she would keep? She loved all of her things. But at her age and with no foreseeable future, if she did put it all in storage, Preston would probably wind up having to sell it all anyway. It was clear she needed help.

Marion sighed and slowly walked over to the large entrance-hall table and picked up the brochure the stager had left for her.

DOWNSIZING?

Call Elegant Estates, a full-service, moving, packing,
and liquidation estate sales company. We do the
work, you sit back, relax, and leave it to us.
Call for a free estimate

The lady on the phone was very accommodating and said, "Oh yes, honey, we will be happy to handle that for you! All I need you to do is figure out which items you want to keep, what you want to store, and what you want to sell, and like we say, we will do the rest!"

The next day two young women from the Elegant Estates and Liquidation Sales Company knocked on Marion's door and introduced themselves as Terrie and Wendy. The minute they entered and looked around the house, Terrie, the one with the pad and pencil, said in a singsongy voice, "Oh dear. I see we have lots of brown elephants here."

Marion looked around and said, "Elephants?"

"Oh . . . I'm sorry. That's what we call all dark-brown furniture. I'm afraid nobody is buying it anymore, and there's not much of a market for the Oriental rugs. People are doing mostly tile these days. And oh, all those garden statues should go too."

Marion had to admit the majority of her furniture was dark brown. The English secretary, the bookcases, all the coffee tables and side tables, the Queen Anne dining-room table and chairs, the buffet, all of it really.

In the kitchen she had at least twelve sets of dishes, six sets of silverware, four silver tea sets, two large silver coffee urns, and all of her handpainted Spode dinnerware from England, including six formal gravy boats.

They had warned her about the dinnerware. "We may not be able to sell these. People don't want things you can't put in the microwave. You might want to think about Goodwill. Some of the paintings are nice, but those framed photos have got to go. Too personal. And the rugs are good, mostly. We might be able to sell a few, but . . . I doubt it. So here are some colored stickers. Blue are for things you want to keep, and red for what you want to sell."

And to make a terrible day even worse, the minute the van with a large sign that read YOU CAN'T TAKE IT WITH YOU. ELEGANT ESTATE SALES, drove away, her neighbor Barbara saw it and came over wondering what they were doing there. Marion had to lie. Marie had told her not to mention that the house was going on the market, or every realtor would be driving by day and night. So she told Barbara they were giving her an estimate for insurance purposes. She would know the truth soon enough.

Later on that afternoon, Marion wandered through the house with her red and blue stickers, heartbroken, as she placed a red sticker on each piece of furniture and said a tearful goodbye to every table, chair, painting, and everything on all the tables—everything she owned, really. She had already donated the piano and the harp to the local theatre group and almost all of her clothes to their costume department.

She had kept a few things to tide her over until the house was sold.

Then there was her jewelry she had to deal with. She did have a lot of fine pieces, and enough strands of pearls to sink a small ship. What to do? Marion stood there and stared at the pearls and thought, Oh the hell with it. I'll just sell them. But she did keep one small strand. Even if her demise was to be soon, she couldn't bear to face what time she had left without at least one small strand of pearls. For old time's sake, if nothing else.

Later she went out to the large garage and placed a blue sticker on her much-beloved midnight-blue 1999 Lincoln Town Car. Or as Preston referred to it, "The Gas Guzzler." Although Bucky, their driver, was retired now, she wanted him to have it. She had enjoyed many a good ride in that car. She patted it on the hood and said, "Goodbye, old girl," and left.

A few days later, after a grateful Bucky had picked up the car, and all of her donations to the theatre group had been delivered, Marion called Elegant Estates and told them she was ready. And almost before she had hung up, it seemed, a small army of worker bees in tan overalls arrived to prepare for the estate sale. The lady in charge of the army said, "Hon, we recommend you not be here while we work gettin' things together. Why don't you take yourself to a nice lunch somewhere?"

Marion picked up her purse and took a cab over to the club. She ordered her usual chicken salad on a half papaya, with sliced almonds, but she couldn't eat a thing. She just sat out on the terrace overlooking the pool, with her heart breaking. This was it. The last chapter in what had been the lovely story of her life. She was about to turn to that last page, the one that read "The End."

Before she left the club that day, as a silent thank-you to the staff, she shamelessly overtipped everyone. With what those poor people had to put up with these days, they deserved anything she could give them.

When Marion arrived back home, all the so-called excess items had been removed and laid out end to end on the long Queen Anne dining table. Everything inside the house, including her bedroom sets, now all had price tags attached.

The thought of total strangers invading her home, rummaging through her family things, made her sick to her stomach. Her poor mother would be turning over in her grave if she knew what was to become of her lovely things. Marion wondered how she would be able to live through the next few days, knowing what was coming. Her lovely home had just been turned into a flea market. At that very moment, all over Birmingham, bright-pink flyers were being posted on telephone poles and slipped under doors.

Come One, Come All! Take home some Treasures!
Estate Sale
214 Crestview
This Saturday, 10 A.M. to 5 P.M.

But life does have its strange twists and turns. On the Friday night before the estate sale, at exactly 2:27 A.M. Marion's neighbor Barbara suddenly woke up to the strong smell of smoke. She frantically poked her husband. "Stan! Stan! Wake up, I think the house is on fire!" Stan sat up and smelled the smoke as well. He jumped up and ran downstairs, with his wife close behind. They turned on all the lights and looked all around the house and were relieved that it was not their house that was on fire. But a few seconds later, they heard the loud roar of windows bursting and the sound of screaming sirens as four fire trucks pulled up next door. They walked outside only to find their poor neighbor Marion standing on the sidewalk in her nightgown, sobbing as she watched her home going up in flames. She kept crying out and wailing "Oh no . . . no . . . My home! My things! Oh no, not my home . . . oh no . . . help me!" Barbara and Stan ran over to her as fast as they could, and Stan caught Marion just as she collapsed in a dead faint on the sidewalk. As they tried to revive her, they were both terrified. They had never seen her looking so pale, and they were afraid she might be dead.

After the paramedics came and were finally able to revive her, they took her to the hospital to check her out. Barbara and Stan rushed back home and dressed and went to the hospital, too, in case they were needed.

An hour later, after a careful examination, the doctors came out and told them that their neighbor had inhaled a great deal of smoke and was now on oxygen to help clear her lungs. They also guessed she must have fallen and hurt her knee running down the stairs in the dark, and they had wrapped it and put it in a knee brace. Other than that, she apparently had suffered no serious, life-threatening injuries. A true relief. Preston flew in the next day to make sure his mother was all right. However, considering the tremendous shock she had just been through, the doctor said she needed to be put into a rehab center to regain her strength.

When Terrie and Wendy over at Elegant Estates were informed of the fire, Terrie said, "Rats, there went our commission."

Marie, the real-estate lady, quickly had a new ad printed:

For sale. Rarely available, beautiful,
one-of-a-kind view lot, overlooking the city.

A few days later, the fire inspector determined that the fire had started in the dining room and had quickly spread through the entire house. He said, "In these old houses where the electrical wiring isn't up to code, it often happens; once fire hits those old circuits, it's all over." They guessed that a worker preparing for the estate sale must have accidentally knocked over one of the large silver cigarette lighters in the dining room, spilling fluid on the rug, and sparks from its old flint had begun to smolder, setting the rug on fire.

The fire inspector told Marion she was darned lucky that she had smelled the smoke when she did. He said if she had come downstairs a minute later, considering how fast the fire was spreading, she would not have gotten out alive.

She didn't care about herself. The thing that mattered to Marion was that the house had been completely destroyed. So many years of happy memories burned to the ground in less than an hour. Nothing left but a pile of ashes, and her memories of a happier time. All that was left was her grandmother's dinner ring that she was wearing at the time.

Marion spent the following few weeks in a blur, trying to go through inventory lists for the house and all of its contents. Luckily, Newton had copies of the household furnishing appraisals in his office at the time of the fire.

Later, after the insurance company finally settled the claim, and the lot went into a bidding war, it sold for over the asking price. Marion was able to give her longtime workers the generous bonuses she'd hoped to give them, and donate to her charities. A week later, Marion packed her few things and headed to Palm Beach, Florida, where several of her other friends had moved. And thanks again to the generous settlement, she was now living in a brand-new, spacious, ocean-view condo.

Life really is so strange and full of surprises. Marion had assumed she would be completely devastated losing everything that had mattered to her, and just not want to live. However, something completely unexpected happened. For the first time in her life, Marion suddenly felt free and unencumbered and was actually looking forward to making new friends.

Looking back now to the night of the fire, it had certainly not been easy for Marion to light that match and take it to the dining-room rug, where she had just emptied the lighter fluid from her silver cigarette table lighters. It had broken her heart to do so, but at least all of her lovely family things had not been scattered all over God-knows-where and pawed through by perfect strangers looking for a bargain. She had absolutely no regrets. She had given her home and her beloved belongings the decent burial they deserved.

At first, she had planned to stay in the house and go up with it, get it over with. But she couldn't do that to her son. So she waited until the last minute to run down the stairs and out of the house.

Yes, she had taken a big chance. And no question about it, she could very well be sitting in jail right now. But thanks to her earlier training in local amateur theatricals, the pale makeup and the fainting on the sidewalk had sealed the deal.

P.S. She still did have that one small strand of pearls. The morning before the fire, she had secretly stashed them in Barbara's geranium pot next door.

Traffic Stop

Officer Vaughan

The minute the highway patrolman saw the car up ahead driving erratically and swerving from side to side, he pulled up behind and followed it. The car kept slowing down, then jerking forward. What the hell was she doing? he wondered. He put on his siren and pulled the car over to the side of the road, parked, and walked over.

The driver rolled down her window and looked at him. "Hello, Officer," she said sheepishly. The driver was a very pretty young woman and had a baby in the backseat, strapped in a baby seat.

"Lady, are you aware that you were driving all over the road back there?"

"Yes sir, and I'm so sorry."

"What's going on? Were you texting while driving?"

"No, Officer, my phone was in my purse. I never do that. What happened was, after I got the baby strapped in, I drove off and forgot to put on my safety belt, and then, when I remembered, I was struggling to get the thing on, and then my cellphone started ringing, and I thought it could be my husband, so I reached for it, and when I did, it dropped and it slipped down under my seat, and I was trying to get it out of there to answer, plus I was having trouble finding the buckle of my seatbelt, which I finally found and got it to snap in place. Then I tried to drive on, but my sleeve got caught in the seatbelt strap and I couldn't get my arm out and anyhow . . . that's probably what happened."

"Uh-huh," he said. Officer Vaughan had heard a lot of crazy excuses in his day, and this was a good one. "Well, I'll need to see your driver's license and your registration. Have you had anything to drink in the last four hours?" He was sure with a baby in the back that she hadn't been drinking, but he had to ask.

"No sir," she said, and handed him her papers. "And Officer, I hope you're not going to give me a ticket. I've never gotten a traffic ticket before. Not one, ever. And I've never even been stopped before."

As he looked at her papers he asked, "And where were you headed, miss?"

"Well, you see, Officer, today is Friday, and I was on my way to my mother-in-law's house. My husband works very hard all week, and we have our date night every Friday night, and she's babysitting for us. We've only been married for two years, and I guess I may have been thinking about our date, maybe, and not paying attention, and forgot to put my seatbelt on, I guess?"

"I see," said the officer. He handed her license back to

her and glanced at the little blond boy in the backseat. "That's a mighty handsome kid you got there, miss."

"Oh, thank you. He looks just like his dad. And if you don't mind my saying so, you are pretty good-looking yourself. So . . . umm, am I going to get a ticket, Officer?"

Officer Vaughan was a little thrown, as the woman had also just winked at him. "No, I'm gonna let you off this time with a warning. But next time, don't start driving before you've put your seatbelt on, okay?"

"Yes sir, I'll remember, I promise . . . Umm, can I leave now?"

"Not yet. I need to do one more thing." Officer Vaughan quickly looked around to see if anyone was watching, then he took off his hat, leaned in the window, and kissed the young, pretty woman right on the mouth, then said, "See you tonight, honey. But be careful, you hear?"

"I will," she said. "Can't wait, bye!" And she drove off.

Of course, he really shouldn't have kissed her while he was on duty. But then, it wasn't every day that an officer pulled over his own wife.

Christmas in Cottonwood

Velma

Velma was up and dressed by six thirty. Felton and Earlene would be picking her up by seven. They needed to get to the Cottonwood Community Hall early and get set up, put the presents out and all the baked goods, and set up the coffee.

They had spent the last weeks decorating the huge Christmas tree and hanging Christmas decorations. The Christmas Eve celebration at the hall had become a tradition, and they went all-out. It was started by the people who had survived the Dust Bowl years and still remembered when the sky was black every day. As one of them said, "There was a time here when we didn't have Christmas, so that's why we tend to overdo it a bit."

This would be Velma's fifty-second year playing Mrs. Santa Claus, and after church, all the children would pile into the hall to get a present from Santa and a cookie from Mrs. Claus. She had to laugh, as she had told Earlene on the phone, Mrs. Claus had to let her red dress out a little more this year. "I weigh the same. I'm not getting fatter, I'm just getting shorter!" Ever since Velma's husband, Dolf, died, Felton Moats had stepped in to be Santa Claus. Over the years, Velma had seen so many children grow up and then come to the Community Hall with their own children. It was always a joyous time of the year, but later when she was home, it was also a time when she missed her daughter, Ruth Ann, the most. If only she had stayed home in Kansas. If only they hadn't lost her to Hollywood.

But Velma had learned a long time ago that if you let it, life can wind up being just an endless list of what-ifs, and why-didn't-I's, should or shouldn't-haves, and why-did-I's. There were times you'd just have to accept what the Good Lord handed you, make the best of what you do have. Besides, we have no choice in the matter.

Velma picked up the phone and called her granddaughter, Cathy. It was still early in California, but nobody was home, so she left a message.

"Ho-ho-ho, this is Mrs. Santa Claus calling for Tracie Ann. Merry Christmas all the way from the North Pole ho-ho-ho."

Beep. *If you are finished with your message you may hang up, or if you wish to—*

Velma interrupted the voice and said, "Ho-ho-ho and a Merry Christmas to you, too, whoever you are." After she hung up, she thought about that poor lady, having to work answering phones on Christmas Eve. Bless her heart.

On Christmas Eve morning in California, Tracie Ann had told her mother she was too excited to wait until

Christmas morning to open her present from Nana. So after a long day of her asking, Cathy finally said, "Oh, all right." Tracie Ann immediately tore into the large box wrapped in smiling Santa Claus faces and was delighted to see that it was the complete set of the original Nancy Drew, Girl Detective books. There was a note inside, which read,

> Your mother loved these books and I know
> you love to read, so I want you to have them.
> Merry Christmas to my precious Tracie Ann.
> Missing you and wish you were here.
> Love, Nana

Tracie Ann always loved getting presents from Nana. Although she had not seen her for quite some time, she still remembered when she was eight, and her mom and dad had let her go and spend the entire summer with Nana at the farm. It had been so much fun. Nana let her hold the baby chicks, and go barefoot whenever she wanted to, and sleep with a big teddy bear, even when her mother said she was way too old to do so. She and Nana even went to outdoor picnics at Nana's church, and a woman friend of Nana's named Earlene had made her a bracelet with her name on it.

Cathy's mother had died long before Tracie Ann was born, but lucky for her, she had her great-grandmother, Nana. And nobody made hot chocolate like her nana.

City of Lost Dreams

Ruth Ann

They had come from all over the country, from every small town, every state. Each day, young hopefuls arrived by the dozens, by buses, cars, or planes. A few even hitchhiked to get there. Some had been encouraged by teachers or friends. Some were told not to go, but came anyway. The glamour and excitement of Hollywood was calling all the bright young singers and dancers, pretty girls and boys, actors and actresses with stars in their eyes, dreaming of fame and fortune, looking for that one big break. That's all they needed. Just one.

Years later, many were still there, living in their small, dark, one-room apartments, too ashamed to go home a failure, too proud to ask for money, too broke to buy new clothes.

The older woman with the slight limp who ushered you to your seat at the Hollywood Bowl had once been the one everybody in her acting class had predicted would make them proud one day. The forty-year-old, slightly balding man, now waiting on tables, was once an excited boy of eighteen who knew he would one day be a movie star.

And Ruth Ann was now just another one of the many lost in the shuffle. Of course, there were moments when she knew she should just give up on Hollywood and go home. Even her third-rate agent had leveled with her and advised her that maybe she should consider another profession. Unlike some others, she did have a place to go. Her mother back in Cottonwood, Kansas, always ended each letter, each phone call, with the same plea: "Please, just come on home, honey. Your daddy and I love you and miss you and Cathy so much." Ruth Ann thought about it. It would be so much easier to raise her child there. Cathy was now getting to an age when she should not be seeing the things she was seeing.

But then, how could she come crawling back to a town she left behind so many years ago, face the sweet boy who had loved her, the one she'd turned down? What could she say to all her friends and classmates she had not kept up with? How could she come back a complete failure after the grand send-off the town had given her, with the banner that read OUR STAR OF THE FUTURE. She was not that girl anymore. The once-beautiful young blond girl with the bright crystal-blue eyes had faded, bit by bit each passing year, until she was just one of a thousand forgettable faces behind a bar pouring drinks for other nameless faces, living in a motel room in Burbank, still waiting for her big break.

But long after her city of dreams became her city of lost dreams, Ruth Ann had held on, until one day she just gave up, leaving behind a trail of broken hearts, including her own. When she died she only had two questions left unanswered. If she had known how her life was going to turn out, would she still have left home? And who or what had selected the small few who had succeeded where she had failed? Had her fate been determined by just the big spin of some huge fortune wheel up in the sky? Round and round she goes, and where she stops, nobody knows.

The High School Reunion

Carolyn

~⚮~

Carolyn Paige had not attended any of her past reunions, but this year, she was going and she was excited about it and terrified at the same time.

This would be their eighth reunion, and it had been that long since she had last seen Kevin Casey. Although she had kept up with him as best she could, reading little things in the local paper about how after graduating from chiropractic school, he had joined his father's practice. But so far nothing about marriage plans.

Funny how life turns out. Never in a million years would she have guessed that the day would come when she would actually want to go to her reunion.

Her high school years had not been happy ones. As a matter of fact, they had probably been four of the unhappiest years of her life. But then, none of her school years had been a very good experience.

Beginning as early as the first grade, Carolyn had been known as the little fat girl and had been nicknamed "Butterball." And the older she got, the more painful it became. Even though she was tall, 5'8", by her freshman year, she had blown up to a very hefty two hundred pounds. Her poor mother had tried everything to help her—diets, taking her to exercise classes—but nothing had worked.

High school was four years of sheer torture. She was an only child, and had been lonesome most of her life, and she wanted so badly to make friends her own age, but it had not happened.

At the school cafeteria she usually sat by herself watching the other kids laughing and having fun, over-hearing them talking about parties to which she had not been invited, watching the pretty, popular girls walking down the hall so free and easy, while she hugged close to the wall as she walked, afraid she might bump into someone and embarrass herself.

Unlike grammar school, nobody at Altmont High was mean to her or called her names, they just didn't seem to see her. Her high school years were spent standing on the outside, watching, trying not to get in anyone's way, longing so badly to just fit in. Wondering what it felt like to be normal. To not be her. To have a boyfriend.

And of course, there was this one boy, Kevin Casey, she had a painful crush on, and to make matters worse, he was the football star, so every other girl in school did too.

Then one day, as she was walking down the hall headed to her next class, she looked up and saw him coming down the hall talking with a friend and they were headed right toward her. Oh no! She desperately looked for a door to quickly step inside and hide, but there were none. And in the process of trying to get out of the way she accidentally dropped one of her books on the floor just as he was passing her. Not missing a step as he went by, he quickly reached down, picked it up, and handed it to her and said with a smile, "Here you go," then walked on by, still talking to his friend. Poor Carolyn had nearly fainted. Kevin Casey had actually looked at her and smiled. The moment had lasted only for a few seconds, but she'd never forgotten it.

It would be hard to pick just one, but her senior year might have been the worst. So many activities to be left out of. So many parties and dances, and of course nobody had asked her to the prom. For her senior yearbook photo, although she usually wore her hair in a ponytail, she tried to wear it long and pull it down on both sides of her face, hoping her cheeks wouldn't look so big. But it didn't work. No surprise, her crush, Kevin, was named Most Likely to Succeed. Under her picture was just her name and the words "Sweet and shy."

After graduation, she had gone to college out-of-state. She never saw anybody from high school again, didn't want to really.

Now she was ready to go back and see everyone again. But it would not be the same old Carolyn going back. It would be the brand-new Carolyn.

. . .

After years of suffering, with weight gain and loss and gain again, fighting diabetes, obesity, shame, and guilt, she was prescribed a brand-new treatment. Over the last few months, and with just one shot per week, the extra pounds she had been hauling around on her body began to slowly melt away and disappear. And soon, like a block of marble becoming a beautiful statue, what stepped out from the large mass of a person she used to be was the one who had been inside of her all of her life. To everyone's surprise, most of all hers, what had emerged was a tall, blue-eyed blonde with cheekbones and long, slender legs to kill for. A Taylor Swift lookalike, her office friend had remarked. In other words, she was a knockout. A real babe. Who knew?

The new Carolyn turned out to be absolutely drop-dead gorgeous.

The night of the reunion, she picked out a simple black dress that showed off her peaches-and-cream skin. She had never wanted to be seen in a bathing suit, and as a result of not ever having gone in the sun, she looked younger than she was. Another surprise.

When Carolyn arrived at the school auditorium, she waited about fifteen minutes after the event had started, then made her entrance. At first nobody noticed her come in, and so she went up to the table to get her name tag. One of her old schoolmates, Janice Clapoff, was sitting at the table.

Janice looked up and said, "Hi . . . can I help you?"

"Hi, I'm here for the reunion."

Janice looked puzzled. "I'm sorry . . . are you sure you're in the right place? This is . . ."

"I'm Carolyn Paige. We graduated together?"

"Who? I'm sorry, the music is so loud. Who did you say?"

They had a copy of the yearbook out on the table, and Carolyn turned it to the page with her picture. "I'm Carolyn Paige."

Janice's jaw dropped as she looked at the picture then back at Carolyn. "No way!"

Carolyn reached over and picked up her name tag and put it on, then said, "Good to see you, Janice," and headed toward the crowd. The loud chatter stopped as she passed by the different groups, making her way to the bar. People just stared. And when she caught their eye, hoping to start a conversation, they quickly turned away.

"Who is that?"

"I don't know."

And Carolyn found herself standing all alone.

Janice had been watching her being stared at and finally got up from the table and walked over to the bar and picked up a glass and banged on it to get everyone's attention.

"Hey, everyone. Let's say hello and welcome back to Carolyn Paige. This is her first time back."

Needless to say, people who actually remembered Carolyn by name were stunned. A few of her old class-mates came over to say hello, but they didn't know what else to say, except things like, "How are you doing?"

"Good to see you again."

"You look terrific."

Most of the girls were married now and had to drag their husbands away as they stood staring at Carolyn.

A few of the single guys standing over in the corner were daring each other to go over and ask her to dance, but none did. One of the guys, Kevin Casey, would sneak little glances at her from time to time and said to his friends, "I don't know who she is, but . . . God . . . she's so pretty, I can't even look at her. Besides, I'm sure she'd never give me the time of day. Man, I sure envy the lucky guy . . ."

Carolyn had spotted him over in the corner and tried her best to catch his eye, but every time he would quickly turn away before she could wave at him. He clearly had no interest in talking to her.

Almost no one had really recognized her, or had really even tried to get to know her. After they said hello, they had just drifted back to their groups. She had not recog-nized a lot of them at first either. Some had put on some weight, and a lot of the boys were going bald now. Those golden teens she had so admired were just average-looking grown men and women now. Except Kevin. He still looked wonderful.

After a while, she realized nothing had really changed. She was still on the outside looking in. Once they didn't see her at all, and now they saw her, but all they could see was this glamorous, beautiful stranger. Someone whose spectacular looks intimidated both the men and the women.

Poor Carolyn was destined to never be a regular, normal person. Which was all she ever wanted to be.

But after having lived through years of misery, and having now lived through the heartbreak of that night, the good news was that Carolyn did eventually find happiness.

A few weeks after the reunion, she went to a Mexican restaurant in the middle of the day and ordered a large margarita. It was not like she couldn't find a man now. All she did was fight off the ones who were chasing her night and day. But it wasn't her they wanted, she knew that. It was just how she looked. And she had to admit, after all these years, she was still in love with Kevin Casey. She sighed and ordered another margarita. Then she gathered up all the courage she had, or probably would ever have again, liquid and otherwise, and walked down the street to his office and into his examination room. "I'm here to ask you out on a date and I won't take no for an answer. This is my phone number. Call me."

Then she said to the patient he had on the table, "Sorry," and turned around and left.

The man looked at Dr. Casey with wide eyes and said, "Whoa . . . was that Taylor Swift?"

After a few dates, Kevin finally got over his shyness and was able to get past her looks and see the sweet, shy, unspoiled girl she really was and always had been. And to his surprise, he became the lucky guy who got to marry her.

And so Dr. Kevin Casey and his glamorous wife had three beautiful children, and lived happily ever after. And all this from his just reaching down and picking up a book. An incident he didn't even recall.

The Cardboard Box

Nancy

Mrs. Nancy Gregory was wandering around the antique store, the one she loved to visit when she was in town for the annual Cherry Festival. The shop was chock-full of old vintage items, and she always found herself wondering about them. The old chairs, the sweetheart pillows, old kitchenware that had once been in happy and loving homes and were now sitting on a strange shelf wearing a price tag. Did they hope that someone would buy them and take them home? Did they miss the lady who used to cook with them? The shelves full of sets of old Dick and Jane books, and the Rover boys, what child had read them and been entertained for hours? Who had loved that Scottie dog doorstop, or the old, faded Raggedy Ann doll on the bottom shelf?

And there was one cardboard box sitting on a table that Nancy was always drawn to. It was a box full of old black-and-white photographs of people in one second of time, life caught on a piece of glossy paper, in a special moment that could never be lived again.

Pictures of people now gone from the Earth, vanished into thin air, nothing left of the laughter and tears, joy and sorrow of their lives but a photo in a cardboard box that a stranger like herself could shuffle through. Who had they been? Who had they loved, who had loved them? How could a once full flesh-and-blood life wind up as just another photograph in a cardboard box? Who was that handsome young man in the bow tie, and the pretty girl with the ribbons? Were they in love that day? They looked so happy. Did they marry? And the old man standing on the porch stairs, had he once been a soldier? A doctor?

What happened to the little girl holding the black-and-white puppy, the mother and baby, the young man standing so proudly by the Model T Ford, the photo of a lake with a blanket laid with picnic food on the ground? And who was the lady in the dark clothes standing so still and staring out at her? The lives lost and gone, and nothing left of them but a black-and-white moment in time. She wondered if they knew life would be so fleeting, and how very important that second in time was, that it would never come again. How could they have known that one day, that special moment in their lives would wind up in a cardboard box, on a table, in a room full of strangers? Nancy wished she had known how fast life passes by. She wished she could go back in time and relive her two children's childhood all over again. But they were both grown now, and busy with families of their own. She had saved some things, her son's old baseball glove, her daughter's first little pair of ballet slippers, all the programs from the many dance recitals throughout the years. She had even saved their report cards, the good ones and the bad. Precious memories to her, but life being what it was, she guessed even those were destined to wind up in a box somewhere. Where did all those memories, hopes, and dreams go, she wondered. After we are gone, do they still linger in the air or do they just fade away forever?

She sighed and continued to roam through the store full of precious memories, ones loved by someone she didn't even know.

Little Church of Signs and Wonders

Billy Campbell

PIEDMONT, NORTH CAROLINA
1981

"How old were you when you got that gunshot wound, Mr. Campbell?" After his regular dermatologist had retired, Mr. Campbell was seeing his associate for the first time. And during the examination the young doctor had noticed the small, round scar on the man's shoulder.

Mr. Campbell glanced over at his right shoulder. "Oh, that . . . oh gosh . . . sixteen, seventeen, I think. Something like that."

Mr. William Campbell, a silver-haired, distinguished-looking man in his mid-seventies, did not seem the type of person to have a gunshot wound, being head of the Chamber of Commerce and a deacon at the church, and one of the city's leading citizens, so the doctor was curious. "If you don't mind my asking, how did it happen?"

"You mean . . . how did I get shot?"

"Yes sir."

"Oh, it's a long story. You probably don't have time to hear it."

"Actually, my next patient isn't due until after lunch, so I do have some time, and I'm just curious."

Mr. Campbell said, somewhat hesitantly, "Well . . . I usually don't tell anybody, it was sort of a flukey thing, really. You see, I grew up in this little country town in North Carolina called Piedmont."

"Oh, I just assumed you grew up here in Charlotte."

"No . . . so my grandmother used to run the local filling station, and it had a little market inside that sold candy, cigarettes, beer, you know, that sort of thing. So after school, I used to go over and help her clean up the place a little, you know . . . and anyhow, this one afternoon, while I was in the bathroom around the side of the building, out of the blue, this guy drives up, walks in, and pulls a gun on my grandmother, and was in the process of robbing her when I came around the front and saw him. Well, I took one look and could see what the guy was doing. So anyhow, it made me so mad, and I went in after him and tackled him from behind. I was on the football team and in pretty good shape, so after I got him down on the floor, we were rolling around and I was trying my best to get the gun away from him . . . and I probably would have shot him with it if he hadn't managed to shoot me first."

"Oh wow," said the doctor.

"Yes, but . . . the good news is, after that, he got up and ran . . . took off without getting a dime.

"So we called the police and gave them a good description of the guy, and they found him a few weeks later over in another county."

"Who was he? Did they ever tell you?"

"Oh . . . from what I heard just some no-good drifter kid, too lazy to get a job, robbing innocent people . . . And I'm glad they got him. He got just what he deserved."

"Mr. Campbell, that was mighty brave of you to go after somebody with a gun like that. You're lucky he didn't kill you."

Mr. Campbell, who was in the process of putting on his jacket, said, "Well, thanks, but I don't know whether it was brave or just a matter of not letting him get away with it. My grandmother was a sweet lady and she didn't deserve to be robbed and scared to death, for God's sake."

"Yes, but still, I'll bet you were quite the hero."

"Oh . . . there was some fuss made about it, you know . . . 'local boy thwarts thief,' and that sort of thing."

"I don't care what you say, that was quite a feat, Mr. Campbell. You're a real live hero."

Mr. Campbell seemed embarrassed. "Well, as I said, I don't usually talk about it, so I'd appreciate if you kept it under your hat, you know . . . It happened a long time ago, and also it sounds a little braggy . . . okay?"

"Oh, of course, I understand. But thanks for telling me."

· · ·

After Mr. Campbell got back to his office and sat down at his desk, he wondered why in the world he'd told the young doctor that story. He had never told anyone about it, even his wife and children. But he figured it's always good for people to hear a story about a real hero in this day and age. And most of it had been true, except for that one important detail. It was Mr. Campbell who had been the robber that day. And during the fight with the boy who was trying to get his gun away from him, the gun accidentally went off and he was the one who got shot. But luckily he had managed to get out the door, jump in the car, and make a getaway before the police arrived. And that was only the beginning of the real story.

What had happened to young Billy Campbell later that day was so unbelievable, so incredible, that even if he were to tell someone, they would say he'd made it all up.

That day way back in 1951, after he'd been shot, Billy had been lucky enough to be able to escape the area before the police arrived. He had driven for miles and wound up lost on some country back road with not a sign any-where. Later, after having lost a lot of blood, he began to feel weak. He guessed he must have passed out, because he woke up after hitting a tree, completely wrecking the car. He managed to pry open his door and he fell out onto the road. As weak as he was, he knew he had to get away from the car or they would catch him for sure. So he crawled down into the woods and went as far as he could and stayed there until dark. As he lay there he could hear the sounds of the night and an owl hooting in a tree nearby. He looked up at the big silver moon shining through the pines and started to cry. He was in terrible pain, and dying all alone in the woods, and it made him so sad. What a rotten deal he had been handed in life. Nobody but his sweet old grandmother had ever really loved him. His daddy was dead. His mother was mean when she drank, which was often, and she'd finally taken off with a boyfriend. He had been living at the state-run school for boys since he was ten, and he needed to get out. He couldn't wait until he was eighteen. The teachers there were all men. He didn't like them and they didn't like him. That's why he had stolen the gun out of the night watchman's locker and stolen his car as well. He was on his way to steal some money, then go to some fancy hotel, like the ones he'd seen in magazines. Then he was going to drink a real cocktail and have a good time, for once in his life. And now here he was, shot to hell and dying all alone in the woods. As he lay there his last thought was, Damn. I never even got to have a girlfriend or anything. Life's not fair.

He then closed his eyes and waited for it to be all over. A little while later, to his surprise, he wasn't dead yet. He opened his eyes and began to hear strange sounds way off in the distance. As he kept listening he realized it was the sound of people singing. But what were they singing? As he listened a little while longer he soon made out the words:

"Let us gather at the river . . . The beautiful, beautiful river."

He knew that song. His grandmother had taken him to church a few times when he was little, but after she died he never went back. But where was the music coming from? Was it heaven? Was he dead after all?

He slowly crawled in the direction of the singing and noticed a faint yellow light way off in the distance. He didn't know why, but he kept crawling until he hit a large clearing in the woods and saw a sign that read:

little church of signs and wonders

Reverend Norman Temple

we save sinners by the dozen

Billy crawled up the little dirt pathway to the church and finally managed to pull himself up the two steps to reach the front door. Then after a moment he gathered up all his strength, stood up, and fell into the entrance of the church just as they finished the last verse of the hymn "Can't Wait to Get to Heaven."

The congregation turned and looked and was startled to see a young man covered with blood, slowly crawling up the aisle toward the preacher, and then he passed out cold. The entire church erupted with the sound of people jumping up out of the wooden pews and rushing toward the young man. When Billy came to, they were laying hands on him and praying, *"God, save this boy. Save this poor boy. Father, save him."*

Luckily, Dr. Robbins, who was in church that night for Wednesday-night service, had his medical bag in his car and was able to tend to Billy's wound.

A day later, Billy opened his eyes in a bedroom he had never seen before, when a lady who was sitting in a chair beside his bed said, "Hello, son. How are you feeling?"

Billy was confused. "Am I dead?"

"No, honey, you just had a little operation. But the doctor says you will be just fine. I'm Mrs. Temple, the preacher's wife. I know you must be hungry. Let me go and bring you something to eat. You just rest, and I'll be right back. So glad you're back with us."

"But where am I?"

"Oh. You're in Piedmont."

"Where?"

"Piedmont, North Carolina, honey. Now, I'll be right back with your soup."

During the next few weeks, Billy lay in bed recuperating at the reverend's house behind the church, and at one time or another every member of the church came by to visit him and tell him how glad they were that he was getting better. And more important, Reverend Temple, a kind and gentle man, would come into his room and spend time talking to him and praying with him. Finally one night Billy said, "Reverend Temple, don't you want to know how I got that gunshot wound? I think I should tell you. I've done some pretty terrible things."

"Well, son, I'm not interested in your past. I'm only interested in your future."

"Yeah, well, you don't understand. I'm kinda no good. I really don't deserve nothing."

"Oh, Billy, you shouldn't say that. Why, from where I sit, I see a fine-looking, intelligent young man with a future full of success. What I want you to know is that God saved you for a reason. He doesn't make mistakes. But it's up to you to find out what that reason is."

Several weeks later Billy had recovered, and after struggling with his decision, he knew what he had to do. He told Reverend Temple he would confess to the authorities what he had done, including stealing the car. He would do his time and start over with a clean slate. The next day was Sunday, and Billy went to church for what he knew would be the last time.

Reverend Temple's sermon that day was entitled: "Is Pride Really a Sin?"

Reverend Temple said that, in his opinion, although pride might be interpreted by some to be a sin, he believed there are certain things one should be proud of, which he called the three C's. Your country, your church, and acts of courage. He then looked right at Billy and said, "We will be losing our Billy for a little while, but we are awfully proud of the progress he's made while he's been with us."

He didn't tell the congregation why Billy was leaving, or where he was going, but before they all left that day, each person came up and wished him luck, saying they hoped he would be back soon.

The next day Billy had Reverend Temple call the police and tell them he was ready to give himself up. Later that afternoon, they came and picked him up. As he was leaving, Reverend Temple said, "Like I said, we are very proud of you, son, and promise me you'll come back and see us sometime." And he slipped a fifty-dollar bill in Billy's pocket. Mrs. Temple handed him a sack of her homemade cookies and said, "Yes, we're awfully fond of our Billy," and kissed him goodbye.

It was the first time in his life anybody had really cared about him, and he turned and waved goodbye to them. As the police car pulled away, Billy fell apart and cried like a baby.

The driver looked at him in the rearview mirror. "That your folks back there?"

Billy nodded. "Yeah . . ."

"Look like nice people."

"Yeah . . ."

Being locked up in juvenile hall for thirteen months was hard, but Billy did his time. The one thing that had kept him going all those long days was thinking how he was going to make Reverend Temple and everybody back in Piedmont so proud of him. The first thing Billy did when he was released was to get a job and save enough money to buy a used car. He bought a new suit and brand-new shoes, and the day before he left, he splurged a little and got himself a fancy haircut so he would look good. He had even saved enough money to buy a present for Mrs. Temple. It was a little string of pink pearls he bought at Woolworths, and he sure hoped she liked them.

He was so excited as he drove down the highway, headed to Piedmont, and soon he found the turnoff and drove down the little dirt road that led to the church.

Billy couldn't wait to see them. He'd been dreaming about this trip for so long. And right after he had visited with Reverend Temple and his wife, he was going to go back to that little filling station to find that boy and thank him. If he had gotten away with that robbery, there was no telling what would have happened to him. And if he hadn't been shot, he would never have wound up at the Little Church of Signs and Wonders. That boy at the filling station didn't know it, but he had probably saved Billy's life.

As he drove down the road, he remembered the pine trees, and he soon saw the large opening of the church grounds coming up. But as he made the turn into the grounds, something was off. He was confused. He stopped the car, got out, and looked around. He was sure this was the spot. But the church was gone, and so was Reverend Temple's house that stood behind the church. There was nothing there but dirt. He walked all around looking, but it was just a large empty lot.

He headed into a little town nearby and walked into the barbershop on the corner, and asked the barber, "Excuse me, sir, can I ask you a question? Didn't there used to be a church somewhere around here called the Little Church of Signs and Wonders?"

The barber nodded. "Oh sure, I remember that. My grandmother used to go there. But it's not here anymore. It burned down."

Billy said, "Oh no . . . when?"

The barber turned to another barber, who was sitting on the bench reading the paper. "Hey, Hank, when did that old sign and wonder church that used to be out on the highway burn down?"

Hank looked up. "Oh gosh. I was still in grammar school, so at least forty years ago."

"Yeah, that's been gone a long time now."

"Are you sure?"

"Oh yeah, my grandmother was real upset over it."

"Oh . . . well, do Reverend Temple and his wife still live here?"

"Who?"

"Reverend Norman Temple? He was the minister at the church."

"No, I don't know who that is. Do you, Hank?"

Hank looked up and shook his head. "No. Don't know him . . . must have been before my time. He must have left, or died by now."

"Hank's right, because if he were still around, we'd know him. We give all our ministers free haircuts."

He looked at the well-dressed, handsome young man standing before him and said, "Sorry we couldn't help you, but, I must say, fella, that's a pretty fancy haircut you've got there. You must not be from around here."

"No, but I was here. What about a Dr. Robbins? Is he still here?"

"Nope, don't know him either. We have a Dr. Girard and a Dr. Schroeder. Sorry."

Billy walked out, now totally disoriented, then drove back down to the area where the church had been and sat wondering. Was he crazy? He knew for sure that this was the exact spot it had been. But had it been some sort of hallucination? Had it all been a dream? Billy felt for the scar on his shoulder. No, that was real, but if the church had burned down forty years ago, how could it have been there just a short time ago? Had he been caught up in some kind of time warp? What had happened?

Then something hit him, and he suddenly broke out in a cold sweat. Had it been some kind of a miracle? He'd heard about miracles taking place back in the old Bible days, but he didn't know if they could happen in today's time. His grandmother was the only person he ever knew who went to church. So she must be up in heaven. Had she sent those people to save him?

As Billy reached the place where the little gas station used to be, he was almost afraid to look. But it was still there. That was real, he had not dreamed it. Whew.

He got out with a dozen roses for the lady and walked inside. It was her, the same little gray-haired lady he had tried to rob . . . He slowly walked up to her.

"Pardon me, ma'am. I came here today to tell you how very sorry I am."

She smiled. "Well, aren't you sweet. You must be one of Dwayne's Marine buddies. So many of you have come here from all over to say how sorry they are."

Billy froze in his tracks when he looked up and saw the photo of the same young man in uniform, hanging up on the wall with a black ribbon around it.

"Would you like to see his medal?"

She reached in a box and pulled out the Medal of Valor.

"The whole town's still heartbroken. But he died saving four of his friends. He died a hero. I see you have flowers for his grave. He's buried at the cemetery right down the street. And God bless you for coming, son."

Billy nodded and said, "Yes, well . . . God bless you, ma'am."

He sat in the car for a while, then drove up the road,

stopped at the small country cemetery. The boy's grave was not hard to find. It was the only one with fresh flowers and was covered with tiny American flags.

Billy stood there feeling so helpless. He'd never gotten the chance to thank Reverend Temple and his wife, and now he would never get a chance to thank this boy for saving his life. What could he do? He needed to do something. And so on that day, while standing at the grave, young Billy Campbell made a solemn vow. He vowed that he would live the rest of his life in honor of this boy. He would live his life the way this boy would have, if he'd just had the chance.

No, Mr. Campbell was no hero . . . but he had met one in his day.

The Pandemic

Velma and Cathy

The phone rang and Velma picked up. "Well, hey there! How are you doing all the way out there in California!"

"Hi, Nana, we're all good."

"Oh, I just hate that ol' Covid thing had to hit, and just when you were getting ready to come see me."

"I know. We're disappointed too."

"And oh, I'm so sorry you had to miss my birthday party. It was over at the Community Hall, and they had the entire place filled with eighty-six balloons, all different colors, and right before I was to blow out my candles, the cutest thing happened. The Cottonwood High School band came marching in the door playing 'Happy Birthday to You.' Oh, we had such a big time. We must have had over a hundred people show up. And guess what?"

"What?"

"I blew out all my candles first try, and you know what I was wishing for? To see my grandbabies. But honey, I got so many presents. Lots of handmade throws, and a cute set of tea towels with a chicken motif. And the little

Boy Scout troop built me a brand-new henhouse and came out and put it up for me. The last one I had blew away in that big storm and oh, I got one of those new watches from my Bible class, that you punch to see the time. But enough about me, how is my darling Tracie Ann? She's grown so, I almost didn't recognize her in that last picture you sent me. I just hate that she's going to be cooped up in an apartment all summer. Can't you send her here to be with me so she can get some fresh air? You know I'd just love to have her."

"That's very sweet of you, Nana, but I really don't think she would be very comfortable there."

"Why not? I've got a big old feather bed upstairs just waiting for her."

"I know, Nana, but especially during her formative years, David and I want her to experience a multicultured environment. And right now I think Tracie Ann might feel threatened by the toxic masculinity of some of the cis men there."

"Oh, for heavens sakes, why in the world would she be threatened by sissy men for? They're not going to hurt her any."

"No, Nana. Cis men. Men who are straight who don't identify as homosexual. Men who . . ."

"I know what that is, we have one right here, works up at the hospital. He was part of the team in the emergency room that got that chair off me."

"Well, I must say I'm surprised."

"Why? His name is Grover, and he's as cute as he can be, he even came to my birthday party. What I want to know is who have you been talking to? Why are you so down on men? Your granddaddy was a man."

"I'm not down on anybody, Nana, it's just that I acknowledge and own our history, and the atrocities that our patriarchal society has committed in the past and continues to perpetrate on women and minorities, and the entire world, really."

Velma thought a moment, then said, "Well, Cathy, all I can say is that you may not like some of them, but men invented lots of things that helped the world too. Don't forget, it was a man that invented the polio vaccine. And just think about it, where would we be if we didn't have electricity? So you mustn't throw the baby out with the bathwater, honey."

Cathy sighed. She knew she was never going to make a point with her grandmother, so she changed the subject. "So, Nana, how are you feeling after your big party?"

"Great, except oh, Cathy, I'm down to my last chicken. Ever since Harry, my rooster, died, Bess is so lonesome out there all by herself. She's an old gal now. I remember when Dolf gave her to me for Easter. That must be over ten years now. She was so little, he had her in a teacup with a tiny pink ribbon around her neck. I really should get me some new chicks, but at my age, I'm scared I won't be around long enough to take care of them. So after old Bess goes, I won't have a thing in the world left to take care of."

"Well, that's good news, isn't it?"

"Not for me, I've had chickens all my life. I wouldn't know what to do without a chicken. So see, just another reason you need to come home, so I can take care of you."

"As soon as we can, Nana."

"Well, hurry up now. I'll be here waiting."

After the phone call, Velma walked out on her porch and sat down on the green glider swing. She was so sorry Cathy wouldn't let Tracie Ann come stay with her. She loved that girl with all her heart, and she worried so much about her being raised in the big city with no backyard.

The sun was very warm and soon Velma began to nod off a bit and dream about the last time Tracie Ann had come to visit. That wonderful summer when little Tracie Ann had crawled up in her lap and Velma had petted her head and told her all about the trees, how they reach out to one another with their roots and hold hands with each other, deep under the ground. And if anything happens to one tree all the others feel it. Then she said to Tracie Ann, "So if you ever get lonesome and think you are all alone in this world, just remember, although you can't see me I'll still be there somewhere, holding your hand."

"No matter what?"

"No matter what."

The Will-O-Wets Take a Trip

They had been teammates on the Willina Women's College synchronized swim team, named the Will-O-Wets, over forty years ago now, and the six of them, Bea, Mary Nell, Essie Rue, Floyce, Cody, and Billie Sue, had remained best friends. They all lived in different places now and most were grandmothers, but no matter what was going on in their lives, come hell or high water, the first week of every June, they'd always gotten together for a girls' weekend. And as it is with old friends, there always seemed to be one who holds the group together, the one who did all the planning, sent out all the cards, and that was Essie Rue. And then there was the star of the group, Bea Ballantine, who was raised on a small cattle ranch outside of Tulsa. Her daddy had her on a horse at five, and by age twelve, she was already winning prizes in barrel racing at the Oklahoma state rodeo. When she had arrived at the college as a freshman, Miss Putnam, the athletics director, had spotted Bea right away. Miss Putnam had been obsessed with old Esther Williams movies, and had her heart set on forming a ladies' precision swim team. The minute she saw Bea make a stunning double-flip dive off the high board, she knew this was the year to try to form a team. The rest of the girls had been picked later, and all were excellent swimmers. Mary Nell could hold her breath underwater for almost three minutes!

Miss Putnam's hunch had been correct. In their senior year, at the state championship precision swim team competition in Tulsa, the Will-O-Wets' smashing routine had been performed to the rousing John Philip Sousa "Stars and Stripes Forever." The girls, all in bathing suits of red-white-and-blue, finished their routine by throwing a twirling Bea straight up into the air and landing her on one leg, with her arm up, in a perfect Statue of Liberty pose. After the big finish, as one judge said, when the entire crowd was standing up on their feet and screaming, they couldn't not give it to them.

After becoming champions, the Will-O-Wets often traveled and performed all around the state. For these special exhibitions, they wore red-white-and-blue sequin-covered bathing suits that Billie Sue's mother had made for them. The sequins made it harder to swim because of the weight and drag in the water, but they looked great, especially at night.

They all agreed that those were the glory days. At every performance the announcer would say in a loud voice, "LADIES AND GENTLEMEN. PLEASE WELCOME YOUR STATE CHAMPIONS FROM WILLINA

COLLEGE IN ARDMORE, OKLAHOMA . . . THE WILL-O-WETS!!!"

Then on Miss Putnam's cue, the six girls would parade out to the side of the pool in single file like show horses, with their noses stuck up in the air, hair slicked back with Vaseline, and stop on a dime. Then, one by one, they would dive into the pool, and proceed to knock them dead with their patriotic routine, every time.

At the end of the year, the girls were excited to travel to California and compete in the national championships. They had hoped to win first place, but at the end of the day, they came in second to the UCLA team, who, truthfully, as Miss Putnam said, were just a little tighter in their routine. But even so, Miss Putnam assured them just how very proud she was of her girls. And winning second place was not bad, considering that "those California gals could practice all year round." Their pool back in Oklahoma was not heated. And then, too, poor Mary Nell had gained that extra five pounds, and that had slowed them down a little.

However, they did not leave California empty-handed. While there, Bea had been spotted by the son of a major movie mogul, and he had pursued her all the way back to Oklahoma. They were married within the year. The next time the girls visited Bea, she was living in one of the big Beverly Hills mansions they had seen on their tour of movie star homes. A few years later, three of the other gals had married local boys in their hometowns, and

Mary Nell had become a physical therapist and married Henry Tanaka, her acupuncturist, and they moved to Hawaii.

Bea's first marriage did not last long, but she did get a very nice settlement, enough to buy what she always wanted, a five-thousand-acre cattle and horse ranch outside of Dallas. Before long she married again, this time to a millionaire oilman whose horse had just won the Kentucky Derby. And soon Bea became one of the leading ladies of Dallas society, sporting the largest yellow diamond ring in the state.

But even so, she remained the good ol' down-to-earth, tell-it-like-it-is Oklahoma gal she had always been.

Even though their lives were busy, every year without fail, the group always sent Miss Putnam a signed card and flowers on her birthday. And they never missed a Will-O-Wets reunion. They never forgot each other's birthdays, or a Christmas. They had all six been in each others' weddings, been there during operations, divorces, and now sadly one funeral, when they lost Billie Sue to cancer.

In the years to come, Bea and three of the others had lost their husbands, and Mary Nell was retired. But on June the first, 2024, they all met up at Bea's ranch in Dallas and were planning to go on a road trip to visit Miss Putnam.

The morning after their reunion dinner, they piled

into a minibus with a cute young driver Bea had hired, and headed up to Ardmore, Oklahoma, and laughed all the way, stopping at the first Cracker Barrel they saw.

They talked about all the funny times and sad times they had spent together, and Mary Nell said, "Girls, do you realize how lucky we are to have been alive at the same time? Just think, I could have been born in another century and never even met you guys."

"Yeah," said Floyce, "that's true. Even if you had been born a few years earlier or later, we would have missed one another. Aren't we lucky to have had each other in our lives all these years?"

They all agreed.

When they arrived in Ardmore, the first thing they did was to go over and visit Miss Putnam at the nursing home to surprise her for her ninety-fifth birthday.

As they walked into the nursing home, a passing stranger might have looked and seen a group of five old gray-haired ladies, one with a walker, going in the door. But what Miss Putnam saw that day as they entered her room were five beautiful young girls in sparkly red-white-and-blue swimsuits. No matter how many years had passed, to her, they would always be her girls.

As Bea had remarked just the day before, "Friends are great, but the ones who remember you when are always the best."

The Fiction Writer

It had been some time since his last book. He had taken his wife on that long-promised river cruise through Europe. Then they bought a little vacation house in North Carolina and had spent quite a lot of time fixing it up.

He had also given up cigars—another promise to the wife—and that had made him so squirrelly, he couldn't have written a word, much less a book. Then he'd been hit with that damn knee replacement that had laid him low for about three months. And then there were those weeks spent in Idaho, fly-fishing with his buddies.

After that, he had spent a couple of months preoccupied with the planning of their youngest daughter's wedding, and at the same time, arranging to get his ninety-six-year-old mother out of one nursing home and settled into another. And so, after having to deal with all the back-and-forth distractions of real life, he was now more than ready to get back to his work. In fact, he could hardly wait. He desperately needed to do what he was put on the Earth to do—write. At least that's what several critics had said. And he could tell by his fan mail that his loyal readers were champing at the bit, eager, ready, and waiting to read his next book. His wife was also glad to see him excited about going to work again, and had his thermos of hot coffee ready to go.

Of course, he was aware that the publishing business had changed quite a bit over the past few years. Many of the books being published now were nonfiction political books, or celebrity tell-alls.

But he was a bestselling author, and his agent had managed to get him a really nice advance, so all systems were go. He already had a few ideas dancing around in his head that he couldn't wait to flesh out. This book was going to be a lot of fun. A good adventure story with lots of unexpected plot twists. He knew that what he enjoyed would do the same for his readers.

He was in such a good mood as he walked upstairs to his writing room. He hadn't been there for so long, but when he unlocked the door and walked in, he realized just how much he had missed it. He loved the big open room, the walls filled with memorabilia, framed good reviews, photos of himself at a few White House dinners, and one of him posing beside a large prize-winning fish he had landed in Key West. There was even the faint smell of cigar smoke lingering in the pine-lined walls. He was home, and at last he felt like himself again.

He poured himself a cup of hot coffee and sat down at his desk. But when he opened his computer, ready to begin, something completely unexpected happened. Like a show horse who balks at the last minute and refuses to jump the next hurdle, he found that he was unable to start. Suddenly his fingers began to tremble on the keyboard, and he broke out in a cold sweat. He felt a dark-gray fear gripping his entire body, and he could hardly breathe.

He had been warned of course about the new rules for writers, and he'd chosen to just ignore them, but now suddenly they appeared in his mind like a cement wall blocking his way forward. It had just hit him.

Damn. As a straight, white male, he could no longer write about just any character he wanted to, and certainly not one of color, or of any other variety of persons with labels, without the threat of being canceled and attacked by critics or angry strangers on the internet. What the hell was he going to write about? He certainly couldn't write anything about a woman. If he had a male character say she was pretty, he would be sexualizing her. Or if he said she was zaftig, he might be accused of fat-shaming or . . . No, he wasn't safe writing a female character, of any kind. So forget that.

What could he possibly write? Lately everybody seemed to be offended by almost everything. Christ, if he couldn't be funny, or write a female character, and could only write from within a narrow straitjacket, he suddenly realized he had nothing to say. There was no story he *could* tell.

Later that afternoon, after a few slugs of his good Irish whiskey, he started to smile.

Ten months later, a fabulous new writer hit the *New York Times* bestseller list. Her name was Felicity Loveborn, whose debut book, *The Heart of a Woman,* was a bold, fascinating story of safari adventure leader Kate Dorsett, who fights the dangerous, criminal ivory trade, saving the lives of hundreds of elephants, and of her two lovers.

One reviewer wrote, "Felicity Loveborn's powerful prose puts one in mind of Isak Dinesen's *Out of Africa.*"

Meanwhile, Felicity Loveborn sat upstairs smoking a cigar, with ideas for at least three more books, and couldn't wait to get started. At around noon, his wife called out, "Oh, Felicity dear. Do you want fries with your burger? I'm about to go out and pick up your lunch."

He quickly opened a window to air out the room, and called down, "Sweet-potato fries, if they have them."

A Doctor's Dilemma

Sam and Jim

Dr. Sam Byram sat in his office wondering what to do. It was hard being a small-town doctor. Most of his patients were friends, and Jim had been his childhood friend. They had grown up together. Played football on the same team. Dated the same girls. Jim had even been the best man at Sam's wedding.

He sighed as he reread all the charts, reexamined his X-rays and Jim's latest CT scan, but it was all there in black and white. These results had caught him completely off-guard. Should he tell Jim the truth, or lie? He had never lied to him before. He sat and asked himself what would be best for Jim. He finally decided what he would do.

He walked out to the reception area and said, "Sarah, call Jim and set up an appointment."

"Sure, if I can find him."

"And oh, make it for later in the day, okay?"

Sarah, who had been with Dr. Byram for over twenty-three years, thought this was strange. He had always wanted to schedule Jim earlier in the day, while he was still sober.

"Bad news?"

He nodded sadly. "Yeah, afraid so."

"Well, I'm not surprised. It's a wonder he's lasted this long. The other night Carl and I were over at the VFW for bingo and when we left there he was, as usual, passed-out cold in the hall. I just feel sorry for Margaret and the kids, having to—"

The phone rang and she picked up without finishing her sentence. She didn't have to. Sam had heard it a hundred times before, from almost everybody who knew Jim. That was the sadness of the thing. Sam knew who Jim was and the man he could have been. He probably knew more about him than Jim's own wife did.

Growing up, Jim had always been the bravest boy in town, always the best athlete and the best and truest friend Sam ever had. Sam felt he owed his career as a doctor to Jim. His life, really. Jim was the one who jumped in the river and pulled him out when he'd fallen out of the boat back when they were kids. Sam had always been small for his age, and not much of an athlete, so having Jim the big football hero, the guy all the other guys looked up to, as his friend, had served him well.

A lot of the cute girls had even dated him just so they could be around Jim.

And then there was that one thing that had happened,

which nobody knew about but the two of them. And for that he would be forever grateful.

Everybody who had known Jim wondered, how did a guy like that wind up a falling-down drunk, losing job after job? Granted, Jim had not had a lot of help from his family. Sam's father, Dr. Michael Byram, had been the highly respected mayor of the town. Jim's dad worked as a handyman and never made much money, so when his mother died, Jim wound up having to go to work right out of high school, to take care of his brother and sisters, while Sam had been off at college. Jim worked as a filling-station attendant, then three years later, he was drafted and sent to Vietnam. And after that, things started slowly going downhill for Jim, and he never seemed to recover.

After his tour of duty in Vietnam, when he and his army buddies landed back in the States, a bunch of protesters were gathered at the dock and started spitting at them, calling them names like "baby killer." That's when Jim lost it. He'd seen too many good guys die over there, and he wound up socking one of the protesters in the face and broke his nose. The guy called a cop over, and Jim got arrested for assault and battery and spent two months in jail before he could get back home. Then when he came back, he found out the girl he loved, the one he hoped to marry, had married someone else. He eventually married Margaret, a very nice girl, but as much as she tried, she couldn't help him with his drinking. Things went from bad to worse, and Jim wound up a sad, bitter man, bumming money off of friends, the one whom everyone avoided.

Sam knew this was going to be tough. He buzzed Sarah. "When you reach Jim, tell him to try and come in sober."

Two days later, Jim showed up and Sam could smell the booze on him, but after they put him in the back room and gave him a couple cups of coffee and two aspirin, Jim seemed to be somewhat alert, so Dr. Sam brought him into his office and closed the door behind him.

Jim spoke first. "I'm not drunk. That ol' prude out there thinks so, but I ain't."

"I hope not, Jim, because . . . I really need you to be with me right now. I've got some bad news, and—"

Jim laughed and said, "Oh yeah, that's why you always drag me in here, to tell me I'm gonna croak if I don't stop drinking and smoking . . . Save your breath, I've heard it all before." He stood up to leave.

Dr. Sam said sharply, "Sit down, Jim. It's too late. I've got your test results, and you have less than six months to live. If you're lucky."

Jim sat back down. "What are you talking about? Is this a joke?"

"No, I wish it were, but I want you to listen to me and hear what I am saying. It's stage four . . . Now, as your doctor, I could recommend chemo, radiation, or even surgery. But as your friend, Jim, I'm telling you it won't help. Just prolong the inevitable. At this point, nothing will cure what you have."

"You're sure about this?"

"Positive. Feel free to get a second opinion, but . . ."

"No, no . . . I believe you. But this is a hell of a . . . Damn. . . . Nothing I can do?"

"Not medically, no. But Jim, there is something I want you to do. And I'm hoping you will." Sam choked up and his eyes suddenly filled with tears. "For God's sake, Jim, please . . . for me, for your family, don't die a drunk. Please, I'm begging you, before it's too late. Sober up and let people see the man I know you to be. You have a chance now that many people don't get. You used to be my best friend and I miss you. I want you back, even if it's for a little while.

"Sorry," Sam said as he wiped his eyes. "I'm a doctor, and as much as I want to save you, I can't. It's up to you. Go to AA, go back to rehab if you have to, just don't die drunk."

"What good is that gonna do? If I'm gonna die any-way, I'd rather be drunk."

"Dammit, Jim, listen to me, it's not just about you. Stop being so damn selfish. Think about your kids. Let them have a chance to get to know you. And Margaret. She's a fine woman. Get to know her again. Think about your legacy. You have a chance to die a sober, decent father and husband. You're a war hero, for God's sake.

Don't die letting everyone down. Give us a chance to be proud of you again. Do you have the courage to at least try? We all love you, Jim."

Jim didn't answer, and then he hung his head and started quietly sobbing. Sam got up and went over and put his arm around his shoulders and let Jim cry, then said, "Will you do it?"

Jim nodded. "I'll try."

"And look, this can be our little secret. Nobody ever needs to know a thing about your diagnosis."

At the end of the day, Jim agreed to let Dr. Sam get him admitted to a treatment center in the next town over, and every Friday afternoon, Sam called and checked on him. So far, he was hanging in. Sam was so glad. He wanted to do something to help. He owed him so much.

As Dr. Sam sat there at his desk, his mind traveled back to that fateful Halloween, so many years ago. He and Jim were still in high school, and that night, both of their girlfriends were at a girls' sleepover party, so they were driving around town looking for trouble, as teenage boys love to do.

Earlier that day, Jim had stolen some beers from his dad's cooler, and after drinking a few, he said, "I know what. Let's drive out to Old Man Richter's turkey farm and get one of his turkeys and then let it loose at the high school, and take off!"

Sam's parents were churchgoing teetotalers, and Sam

was not used to drinking, but after a few beers that sounded like grand fun. Besides, nobody liked Old Man Richter anyway. He was mean to his dogs, and not very nice to his wife either. And every Halloween, he always turned out all his lights so he didn't have to give out candy. So Sam figured it wouldn't be too big a sin to steal one of his turkeys.

As they pulled up, sure enough the house was dark, so they went down the back alley and stopped by the barn where the turkeys were kept. Jim looked at Sam. "I double-dog dare you to go in and get one of them."

Sam said, "Why do I have to get it?"

"Because, I'm the one driving."

"What if it bites me?"

"It's not gonna bite you. Are you too chicken?"

Sam didn't want Jim to think he was a coward, so he said, "No, I'm not chicken," and even though he was scared he got out and climbed over the fence, crept over to the barn, and slowly cracked open the door.

The turkeys were quiet at first, so he walked in and grabbed one, and then all hell broke loose. One hundred and fifty turkeys followed him out of the barn, gobbling at the top of their lungs. He tried to climb back over the fence with the turkey under one arm, but as he did, his belt got stuck and he was caught hanging. Suddenly, all the lights in the house and in the yard were switched on and Jim jumped out of the car and pulled Sam over the fence and both jumped into the car. Jim, in his haste, threw the car in reverse, knocking the entire fence down, and now all one hundred and fifty gobbling turkeys were scattering in all directions.

Old Man Richter came flying down his back stairs, chasing after them as they took off up the alley. But not before the old man saw them and immediately called the police to report, "Two of them little town hoodlums just crashed into my yard, destroyed my fence, and stole all my turkeys. And one of them was that Jim Wilson boy. I recognized him."

Jim drove them back to town, all the while looking in the rearview mirror to see if the police were after them, and then he said to Sam, "Listen, if they catch us, you keep your trap shut, ya hear? We could go to jail for this, and I don't want you arrested. And I mean it. I don't stand a chance at going to college and you do. Your daddy's got the money to send you, so . . ."

"Not a chance, Jim, that's not fair to you."

Jim checked the mirror again. "Yeah, it is. I'm the one who dared you. I just never thought you'd do it, you dumbass . . ." Then he pulled over to the curb and stopped the car and said, "Now, get out of here. Or I swear to God I'll pound you . . . Go!"

"Aww, Jim . . . no."

"And don't tell nobody you were with me. If you do, I'll tell them you're lying, trying to look like a big-shot." Jim then made a fist and said, "You better go, or . . ."

Sam reluctantly got out, and Jim took off and left him

standing there. Within less than a minute Sam heard the siren and saw the police car whiz by.

Later that night, Jim was arrested and taken to jail, and Old Man Richter identified him but said, "There was two of them."

Jim said he'd been by himself.

It was in all the local papers. Jim was suspended from school and had to work out at Richter's farm to pay off the cost of the lost turkeys. He never went back for his senior year. Sam was accepted at college only three weeks later, and nobody but the two of them knew that the mayor's son had been there that night. To this day, Jim had never said a word to anyone about it.

A month after Sam told Jim of his diagnosis, Jim showed up at Sam's office, directly from the treatment center, clean, sober, and ready to do what was next. Dr. Sam was amazed at how good he looked. "You look great . . . but how are you feeling? Any pain?"

"No. Nothing yet, other than the usual old football stuff."

"Okay. But do keep checking in with me."

"I will . . . Well, Sam, thanks to you, I'm headed home to see Margaret and the kids, so wish me luck."

"Good luck. Really proud of you."

After Jim left, Sarah walked into Sam's office. "Wow . . . he looked like a different person. What did you give him? I want some of it."

"Nothing . . . He just decided to sober up."

"Well, let's hope he keeps it up. Lord of mercy, I remember him in high school. He sure was a good-looking thing."

A few weeks later, Jim got a steady job from one of his old high school football teammates who owned the local hardware store, and was doing quite well.

And a little while later, what a surprise it was to everyone there when Jim walked into the PTA meeting with his wife, sober.

He was so glad to get to spend time with his sons, get to know them, and soon he began coaching the boys' basketball team on the weekends.

As the six months were almost coming to an end, Sam was getting nervous. He had to call Jim in to be retested.

While Jim was waiting for the results, he was a wreck. He wanted just a few more months. He almost didn't show up to get his latest report.

Dr. Sam walked in with a puzzled look on his face and said, "Well, Jim, I've looked at everything. Twice. And it appears that you are cancer-free, my friend."

"What?"

"Your X-rays are completely clear. I don't know how you did it, but congratulations."

Jim jumped up, ran over and hugged Sam, and ran out the door.

. . .

After Jim left, Sam smiled. He knew that what he had done was unethical. But he was in the business of saving lives. So six months ago, when he lied to Jim about having terminal cancer, he had meant it for Jim's own good. When the real results of Jim's tests had all come back negative, he'd been surprised. Given the way he had been abusing himself all these years, Jim was still in pretty good health. Not at all what Sam had expected. But Dr. Sam knew that if Jim had continued to drink like he did, it was just a matter of time for him anyway. So in a way, he had saved his life. Of course, he had to scare the hell out of him to do it, but he got the results he wanted. Jim went back to being the old Jim, the great guy he had known.

And the biggest surprise of all: Six years later, having established himself as a good, hardworking citizen, Jim Wilson, former town drunk, ran for mayor of the town and won the election. Even Sarah the receptionist voted for him!

Hunter College

Valerie Coleman

Valerie Coleman was in her freshman year of college. On this particular chilly day in October, she had her books in her lap and was struggling to get her wheelchair up a rather high ramp, trying to get to her next class on time, when she heard a voice behind her.

"Here, let me help you." And Valerie felt herself being pushed up the rest of the way. As they reached the top of the ramp she turned to look at the man who had helped her, and was shocked to recognize one of her professors. Dr. Israel Greenwald. He smiled at Valerie as he let go of her wheelchair and said, "I don't want my best student to be late."

Valerie had been so stunned that she hadn't said thank you. The kindness in his eyes as he spoke to her had overwhelmed her. It was kindness without pity. Something she had not seen before. Although Valerie had been the apple of her father's eye, all of the other males she had come into contact with at school—teachers or students—had always looked at her differently. They saw a heavyset Black girl wearing glasses and confined to a wheelchair as something to be pitied, or else they looked past her and ignored her completely. But Professor Greenwald had looked right at her with genuine affection. His was a large class, and this was the first time he had spoken directly to her.

From that moment on, she was in love.

Professor Greenwald was a short, balding man who dressed in tweeds and bow ties and smoked a pipe. Nothing out of the ordinary. But to Valerie, everything about him was fascinating. The way he stood and crossed his arms when he was listening to a student, the way he often took his glasses off and cleaned them, holding them up to the light. She began to fixate on his hands. She watched them as they moved, the way he sometimes twisted his wedding ring, the way he wrote on the blackboard. Each day she couldn't wait to get to his class and had to sometimes force herself not to go into his classroom too early. He was a source of endless wonder to Valerie. Although he was always amusing the other students with his dry and humorous remarks, she and she alone could see how deep his feelings were, how passionate he was about teaching. She hated the way the other students would rush up to his desk after class and besiege him with questions, taking up all his time.

As the year progressed, their unspoken connection began to develop. Slowly at first, nothing overt, just subtle things that went between them. When a student said something particularly stupid, he would sometimes catch Valerie's eye, for just a second, as if to say, *Do you believe what I have to put up with?* He would walk by her desk and pause, and sometimes knock on her desk to make a point. Or when he called on her, he would say, "Miss Coleman, enlighten the ignorant masses with the correct answer, please," and then turn his back on the class as she spoke.

Anything he did thrilled her. She would think about it, dream about it, but she never approached him. She was too shy to speak to him directly.

Then, one day near the end of the semester, he walked past her desk and offhandedly said, "Valerie, don't leave today until I've talked to you, okay?" And he went on by, continuing his lecture. For the rest of the class, all she could hear was the sound of his voice saying *don't leave today until I've talked to you.*

When the class ended, three or four students rushed up to his desk, as usual, and he answered all of their questions. When they left, he looked over and saw her still sitting there and said, "I'll be right with you, Valerie." He gathered his things and put them down, walked over, and sat on the desk in front of her. He studied her eyes for a few seconds, as if he were searching for something, and then he said, "How are you doing, Valerie?"

She managed a weak "Fine."

He said, "No, how are you *really* doing? Are you getting along okay?"

Valerie couldn't look at him anymore. She could hardly breathe.

He sat there and studied her face a few more moments before he spoke. "You know, I worry about you. I know it must be hard for you here. But you're doing great." He reached over and took her hand and held it. "You're all right, Valerie, and if anything is ever bothering you, or upsetting you in any way, I want you to tell me. All right? Promise?"

Valerie managed a nod. Just then, two giggling girls entered the room for his next class and he stood up and patted her on the shoulder. "You're all right, Valerie," he repeated, and walked away. She sat there for a while, still feeling his hand holding her hand.

For the next three years, long after he was no longer her professor, she would sometimes struggle up that ramp just to go by his classroom, so she could hear his voice, but he never saw her there, never knew she had passed by his door.

There was no sexual affair between the Black girl in the wheelchair and the middle-aged, married professor. No breaking of conventions. A brief moment, a brief touch was all there was to it. But even today, so many years later, she could close her eyes and see him across from her, hear his voice and still get a warm feeling, still feel the bittersweet pain. It wasn't much as far as a love life goes, but she still remembered it as if it had happened yesterday. Valerie knew all about unrequited love, and after all this time, when she was alone at night, just the thought of Dr. Israel Greenwald could make her smile.

Dr. Greenwald had passed away long ago—but he would have been proud to know that one of his favorite students had just been elected governor of her state.

Cathy and Velma

❧

COTTONWOOD, KANSAS
JANUARY 1, 2023

Velma could hardly wait for the phone to ring. Cathy had told her that now that she felt Covid was mostly over, they might be coming to see her in the spring, and she said that she would let her know for sure today. As soon as the phone rang, Velma picked up on the first ring.

"Happy New Year!! Are you coming?"

"Happy New Year to you too, and yes, it looks like we are, Nana."

"Oh honey, whooppee! I'm going to get to see my family and my precious Tracie Ann. I'm ready to just squeeze her to death. How soon are you coming?"

"Well, if things keep going as they are, we are thinking the beginning of May."

"Oh, wonderful. My flowers are so pretty then, and I'm sure my pretty yellow butterflies will still be here."

"But Nana, before we come, there are a few things I need to ask you first. We would be renting a Chevy Volt, so we need to know where your nearest charging station is."

"Oh. Hold on, Cathy. Let me run and get a pad and pencil and write all this down."

While she was waiting, Cathy heard some strange sounds in the background.

After a moment Velma picked up again and said, "Okay, I'm back."

"What's that noise I'm hearing? Like something scratching?"

"Oh, that's just my chicken, Bess. She comes in sometimes and visits me."

"Nana, you let a chicken walk around in your kitchen? Doesn't she make a mess?"

"Oh no, she's house-trained. Now, what was it you needed again, honey? Something for the car?"

"A charging station."

"I can tell you that right now, there's a Chevron station next to the post office."

"No, no, we need an electric-car charging station."

"Oh . . . Okay . . . electric."

"And also, Nana, try and find out if there's a store near you that sells gluten-free products."

"Well, I don't know what a gluten is, but I'll sure ask. How do you spell it?"

"G-L-U-T-E-N."

"Okay. Got it."

"Also, see if they sell bottled water and, if so, what kind."

"Bottled water?"

"Yes, in a glass container, not plastic."

"Oh, honey, you don't need to buy any water. I drink plain old tap water out of the faucet. I've got plenty of good water here."

Cathy was appalled at the thought of her grandmother drinking out of some rusty old kitchen faucet, but before she could say anything, Velma changed the subject.

"Oh Cathy, I just have to tell you, everybody here's so excited that you're coming, they're going to throw a big 'welcome-home' party for you over at the church, and we're gonna have so much good food, with lots of fried chicken, country-fried steak with gravy and biscuits, and Earlene is making us a big pot of her chicken and dumplings. Myrtis is doing her apple pie with homemade ice cream, and all kinds of good things."

Cathy winced. "Oh Nana, I'm so sorry, but we don't eat meat."

"You don't?"

"No, nor eggs or fish. We're vegan and we don't do sugar, dairy, or white flour either."

"You don't eat sugar?"

"No, and really, Nana, you shouldn't either. It's not good for you."

"Lord, honey. What do you eat?"

"Mostly plant–based foods."

"Oh dear." Velma looked out in her yard. "Well, I have plenty of plants here, but it doesn't sound all that healthy to me. I think you need a little meat once in a while.

Earlene says all the women in California are too skinny. You're not getting too skinny, are you?"

"No, but I do try to stay in shape. I try and bike at least five miles a day. More if I can. Do you do any exercising?"

"Well, I walk up to the mailbox and back, every day except Sunday. Oh my . . . now I'm worried the big do we were planning won't be fun for you if you can't eat anything but plants."

"Don't worry, Nana, we'll still have a good time I'm sure. And seeing you will be our fun."

"Well, thank you, honey."

Cathy was not looking forward to the next part of the conversation, but it must be had. She took a deep breath and began. "Now, Nana, before we come . . . there's something else you need to know."

"Oh no, what else can't you eat? Don't tell me you don't drink coffee. I just laid in four big cans of Folgers."

"No, it's not about coffee . . . It's about Tracie Ann."

"Oh, well, you tell her I just can't wait to see her again. How is my little angel? Is she still working at the Starbucks?"

"Yes, but now I'm going to tell you something, Nana, and I don't want you to be upset, but . . . Tracie Ann is now a they."

"Tracie Ann is gay?"

"No, Nana, she's not gay, although there's nothing wrong with that, but Tracie Ann is now a 'they.'"

"A *they*? They what?"

"She identifies as they/them."

"I don't understand. What is a they them?"

"Tracie's preferred pronouns. In other words, Nana, they are nonbinary, genderfluid."

"Ginger what?"

Cathy sighed. She knew this was not going to be easy. "Well, let me try and explain. About a few months ago, she . . . uh . . . they . . . told David and I that they had something very important they needed to unpack about themselves. That they felt like they were not a man or a woman, but both."

"Good heavens . . . Well honey, she's probably just going through some little phase."

"No, Nana, I don't think so . . . and also, I wanted you to know that when we do come, they look a little different now."

"How so . . . has she gotten even taller?"

"Yes, a little bit . . . but just so you are prepared, they now dress in men's clothes."

"Oh well . . . I wouldn't worry any about it, your mother always ran around the farm in overalls."

"No, Nana, it's a little more than that. They now have their hair cut at the barbershop."

"What? Oh Cathy, don't tell me she got all that pretty hair cut off. Why would you let her do such a thing, a pretty girl like that? What happened?"

"I know it feels difficult, Nana. David and I are in therapy in order to successfully adjust, but the thing is, Nana, if we come, we need to make sure we use the proper pronouns in order to make them feel comfortable."

"Well, I'm not sure I'll feel comfortable calling my granddaughter they. Put Tracie Ann on the phone. Let me to talk to her."

"No. No Nana, I promised I would call you first and make sure you would honor their preferred . . . Nana? Are you still there?"

"Yes, I'm still here."

"And there's something else . . ."

"Ohhh, I'm afraid to even ask. What else?"

"Their name is no longer Tracie Ann. They prefer the name Garland."

"Garland? Like a garland of flowers?"

"Yes . . ."

"Good Lord, you can't eat or drink anything, and now Tracie Ann thinks she's two different people and is somebody named Garland? Her birthday is in three weeks. How am I supposed to shop for a they or a them? Now I just don't know what to do."

Cathy decided she would wait a while to tell her that Garland now had a small tattoo and a nose ring. Too much information for now.

After the phone call, Velma went out and looked down at her chicken. "Oh, Bess . . . I'm all confused . . . I just don't understand the world anymore."

About three minutes later, Velma's phone rang again and it was Earlene. "Hey, did you hear from Cathy?"

"Yes, she called me."

"And? Are they coming?"

"To tell the truth, Earlene, I don't know. I'm just a little discombobulated at the moment."

"What's going on?"

"Well . . . I thought I had a great-granddaughter, but now it looks like I've got a great-granddaughter and great-grandson, all in one."

"What?"

"Cathy says Tracie Ann thinks she's a boy and a girl all at the same time."

"Is she kidding?"

"No! She said Tracie Ann is now a 'they' and a 'them' and calls herself Garland, and she has her hair all cut off and dresses in boys' clothes. And not only that, they don't eat anything but plants. They don't even eat sweets. No candy, no cookies, nothing."

"What?"

"I know, Earlene, I'm still trying to understand it. I don't know what to think."

"Well, I think they need to get out of California ASAP. What else did Cathy say?"

"She said when they come I need to use Tracie Ann's . . . preferred pronouns."

"Oh Lordy . . . Well, Velma, what are you going to do?"

"What can I do, Earlene? I wouldn't want to hurt Tracie Ann's feelings for anything in this world. So I guess I'll just try my best, but I'm worried to death. Half the time I can't remember where I put my glasses. How am I going to remember I can't say 'her' or 'she,' and have to say 'they' or 'them' and call Tracie Ann Garland? What if I mess it up?"

"Well, Velma, it's a dilemma all right. Lordy, Lordy, Lordy . . . I guess all you can do now is to try to learn her new names."

"How can I do that?"

"Let me think on it, and I'll call you back."

After she hung up, Velma realized she had lied to Cathy about Bess being house-trained. She wasn't. But she guessed she would just have to cross that bridge when she came to it.

Five minutes later, Earlene called her back. "Velma, I thought of a solution, how you can beat this thing."

"How?"

"I'll come over to the farm a couple of times a week and pretend to be Tracie Ann. And you can practice on me, calling me Garland, and they and them."

"Oh thank you, honey. That would be a big help."

"Well, what are friends for, I say. And just so you know, you're not alone, the same thing happened to Cher. I read in *People* magazine that her daughter, Chastity, is now a boy called Chaz."

"You don't mean it."

"That's what I read."

"Oh, Earlene, I just can't keep up anymore."

"I'm right there with you, Velma. Sometimes I feel like I went to bed in one world and woke up in another. Now they force you to do everything online, and you can't get a real person on the phone to save your life. Hell, if I wanted to talk to a machine, I'd talk to my vacuum cleaner. And I'm just about ready to sling my computer out the door. I've got so many passwords, I can't remember which goes with which, and they keep changing everything. I tell you, Velma, some days I get so frustrated, if there was a building tall enough in Cottonwood, I'd probably jump off of it. Anyhow, honey, that's enough whining from me. I'll be out to the farm later on this afternoon and we'll get started on our project."

"Earlene, you're a real friend, and I really thank you for taking the time to help me with this."

"Why, Velma Vanderhoff! After what-all you have done for me down through the years? And don't you worry, honey, we'll get through this, you just wait and see. We might as well face it, it's just not our world anymore."

"No . . . I guess not."

"It belongs to the young now, and I say, if you can't beat 'em, you might as well join 'em, right?"

"Right."

"Hang in there!"

"I'm trying."

A month later Velma went to her mailbox and found this letter:

Dear Nana,

Thank you so much for my birthday gift. I sure can use this money.

I am saving up to buy a new Apple watch. I hope you are really well.

Tons of Love,
Garland (They/Them)

A week later, Garland received a note postmarked Cottonwood, Kansas:

Dear Garland (they/them)

I hope you had a very wonderful birthday. Your mother tells me you are doing so well in school and I am a very proud great-grandmother!

Tons of love back to you honey, Nana (Just/Me)

P.S. Can't wait to see you this spring!

January, February, and March passed—and sadly, Cathy and her family didn't make it to Kansas before Earlene

Moats called Cathy and informed them that Velma had passed away in her sleep the night before.

Two days later, Cathy picked up a voicemail that had come in that morning.

"Hey Cathy, it's Earlene Moats calling again. Listen, I know you can't travel yet because of this Covid thing going around again, but I don't want you to worry about Velma's service. Our church is handling the whole thing, and Felton and I had keys made and we went out and locked up the farm, and so it's ready whenever you might get here. Oh, and we picked up Bess, her chicken, and have her at home with us till you can get here. Now, Felton said he could also have her flown out to you, if you wanted, but he's not sure she could survive the trip. Just let us know."

When Cathy first heard that Nana had died, she'd been completely devastated. And for weeks afterward, whenever she thought about her, she just broke down completely and sobbed her heart out. Her poor, sweet grandmother who had never had more than a ninth-grade education, never had a career, never traveled. Just lived a sad and empty life spent talking to chickens. A life without any purpose or accomplishment. Cathy was so grateful she had been born when she was. When women were allowed a voice. A chance to make something of themselves. To make a difference in the world. Poor Nana never had that chance. What a sad and pitiful, wasted life.

Meanwhile, across the country in a small cemetery, was a simple gravestone that read:

Velma Ruth Vanderhoff

1934–2023

LOVED BY ALL

Two Years Later

Garland

BERKELEY, CALIFORNIA

2025

After Velma passed away, and thanks to Felton and Earlene Moats, her granddaughter, Cathy, had rented the farm to a nice young couple, Jennifer and Patrick Walsh, who, as Earlene said, "Just love chickens, and even have some fancy ones, and one that had won first prize at the county poultry show!"

A lot of things had changed in the past year. Much to Cathy's amazement, the game of cornhole had somehow made its way to San Francisco, and Garland was now the captain of the Starbucks team, and quite good at it.

Garland, now an attractive five-foot-seven teenager with short, blond, curly hair, seemed to be popular with everyone, young or old, and was still living at home this summer, waiting to go to Stanford University in the fall to study medicine, hoping to become a medical scientist with an emphasis on neurology, studies of the brain and all its functions. Or a forest ranger. Either profession would be fine because Garland dearly loved trees, especially California coastal redwoods. The future was wide open with all sorts of exciting possibilities.

One morning in early July, after Garland had bounced out of the apartment, cheerfully headed for work, Cathy turned to her husband and said, "I'm telling you, David, it's the same thing every day. Happy as a lark, without a care in the world, no matter what's going on. I just don't understand it. I was miserable when I was that age."

David looked out the window at Garland walking down the street waving and smiling at everybody. "I know. I thought teenagers were supposed to be moody."

"I did too." Cathy sighed. "I don't know how it happened, but I swear to God, I think Garland is getting to be more and more like Nana every day."

It was true. Garland was one of those rare creatures who loved the world and everything in it, and all these many years later, had not forgotten Nana's story about the trees reaching down and holding hands with each other. Now, with so many new innovations and different ways to communicate with online friends around the world, it felt sort of like the trees holding hands. Only better! Everybody could get on Zoom and talk with people living all over the globe. Garland already had friends in Africa, India, China, and was learning so much about how they lived. How could anyone ever be sad or lonely when you're able to visit with so many friends? And everybody was so great! Just great!

Every morning Garland could hardly wait to get to the computer to find out about all the wonderful new things that were happening in the world. Medical science was making new leaps and bounds in discovering new cures, new ways to help people who were suffering with mental illness, Alzheimer's, substance abuse, blindness, deafness, and obesity. How amazing to be able to read about all the upcoming cures that were just around the corner. Pretty soon, maybe little children would not have to die from cancer, or any other disease for that matter. Garland also carefully followed the daily progress of space travel with great interest and hoped to one day take a trip to Mars or some other planet. Who knows?

From the very beginning, Garland had been in awe of that thin silver computer. Inside that thin, little box was all the information in the entire world at your fingertips, just waiting for you to click on it, and learn about anything you could ever want to know. What a wonderful time to be alive!

What must life have been like before there was the internet and computers or social media? People must have been bored out of their minds!

Garland was never bored for a second, and for the last month or so had been extremely busy studying the many thousands of different species of birds. Just yesterday afternoon, Garland had walked into the kitchen and said to Cathy, "Mom, it just boggles my mind."

Cathy asked, "What?"

"Just think about it. I mean, what kind of a brain could have thought up so many millions of different things? All the different plants, and trees and animals and stuff, and people. I'm studying fish next month, and I can't wait. Hey, maybe I could go to Hawaii and learn to scuba-dive so I can see them in person. Wouldn't that be fantastic? Nana left me that money, and she said for me to use it to have a good time."

"Yes, that's true, she did."

"Hey Mom, how old was Nana when she died?"

"She had just turned eighty-eight."

"Wow. That's so young. Too bad she couldn't have hung on a little longer. Did you know that with the employment of generative AI, pretty soon we will be able to fabricate brand-new artificial hearts, and lungs, livers, pancreases, or anything you need? Something wears out, you just get another. Isn't that great? Wow, I plan on living to be at least a hundred and fifty . . . or maybe more."

Garland suddenly looked at the time and said, "Oops, gotta go, Mom. Got a Zoom call all the way from Australia coming up. See you later."

After Garland left, Cathy shook her head and had to smile. She thought to herself, "With Nana up there, still pulling the strings, I wouldn't be surprised if Garland did make it to one hundred and fifty!"

I Never Said Goodbye to Mama

Clayton

᪥

NASHVILLE, TENNESSEE

2022

Clayton Perkins couldn't go to a public place without being hounded by fans and young would-be stars wanting to know how he did it. Today he sat drinking all alone in the den of his six-thousand-square-foot mansion on Travis Lake outside of Nashville. And as usual at this time of day, he was drunk on his ass, trying to write a new song.

Clayton had not had a hit in years. He was part of old Nashville now. All the new, young, up-and-comers, mostly from L.A., had taken over the country music scene. It was a new world, and he was no longer a part of it. So like so many living legends of the past, he sat remembering all his life's regrets, one by one with each sip, until his biggest regret, the one he never talked about, slipped out on paper as he started to write some lyrics:

> *Had me a ten-dollar guitar and a nice-enough smile.*
> *Took off for Nashville, gonna show 'em my style.*
> *Runnin' wild, in and out of honky-tonk bars,*
> *Chasin' pretty women, tryin' to be a big star.*

I'd been gone near a year when Daddy called,
Sayin', son, come on home, Mama ain't doin' good at all.
Said, "Daddy I'll get there, but see I come this far.
Got a date to record a song, it could make me a star."

Days turned to weeks, a young man's time it flies by.
My song shot up those charts, it had made me a star.
Never stoppin' to think, just jumpin' in for the ride.
Drivin' big fancy cars, pretty women by my side.

Called home one day sayin', "Tell Mama I'm comin' home."
Daddy said, "Sorry to tell you, son, but your mama's gone.
She tried to hang on, but the Lord took her out of her pain.
And the last thing she did, was to call out your name."

CHORUS:
I never said goodbye to Mama.
Now all of my fortune and all of my fame
Can't buy me back what's gone forever.
Left with just myself to blame
I never said goodbye to Mama,
And the last thing she did was to call out my name.

I got the applause and the whole world is mine.
But friend, I'd give it all up, if I could go back in time.
Sittin' beside Mama, just a'holdin' her sweet hand.
I may be a star, but I'm not much of a man,
Cuz I never said goodbye to Mama.

Clayton's agent had been told by all the new record companies that nobody wanted that old-timey, corny, crying-in-your-beer kind of stuff anymore. But because of who he used to be, they recorded "I Never Said Goodbye to Mama" anyway.

The week the song was released, and men were hearing it on the radio for the first time, long-haul truckers from Alabama to Maine were pulling their big rigs over to the side of the road to call their mothers. Many just stopped to have a good cry. A few days later, as the song gained popularity all over America and as far away as Canada, sheet-metal workers, construction workers, and two-hundred-fifty-pound football players were sitting in bars, thinking about their mamas. And much to the surprise of new Nashville, Clayton Perkins was suddenly back on the top of the charts. The song was recorded in Spanish, French, and Italian and the latest request had come from India.

Yes, times may change, people are either in or out of style, but one thing that never changes is men and how they feel about their mamas.

Last we heard, Reba McEntire's people were looking at a song:

"Oh, How I'm Missing My Daddy Tonight."

I think it could be a hit . . . don't you?

A Mother's Secret

Marjorie

⚜

DAYTON, OHIO
2014

If you were to see her out and about in town, you would have never guessed in a million years that Mrs. Marjorie Neale of Dayton, Ohio, an attractive lady with her short silver hair in a stylish feather cut, had a secret. It was not the sort of thing you could disclose about yourself without being thought of as pretty strange. And she certainly couldn't tell her husband, Jim. He was such a normal and devoted father.

It had even taken years for her to finally admit it to herself, and it had come as a complete shock to her. Before then, it had never occurred to Marjorie that such a thing was even possible. And if so, she'd certainly never heard about it.

The secret she had been harboring for the last twenty-five years was that as hard as she had tried, she just did not particularly like her own children.

In fact, if she had just met the two of them for the first time, she wouldn't have chosen to be friends with either one. Not a happy situation, considering they were her two closest living relatives.

She wondered how in the world this could have happened. Had they somehow been switched at birth? One of them, maybe, but two? Not likely. And then, too, they both did have the Neale ears, and her hazel eyes. They were hers all right.

It was truly baffling. And the ironic thing was that she was the one who had actually been looking forward to having children. Jim had just gone along with it. Before they were born Marjorie had just assumed that they would all live happily ever after, with lots of fun trips to Disneyland and family Christmas cards with photos sent to friends, cheerful evenings at home, watching her happy son and daughter at play. But family life had not been what she had expected. Her two children had been at odds with each other from the very start, always fighting and accusing her and Jim of having a favorite. Even at Christmas or birthdays, it always ended in a fight. If one got more presents, or had a bigger party, the other one would have a fit. What they did for one, they always had to do for the other. If they sent one to camp, they had to send the other, and on and on.

How could this have happened? She had tried her best to do all the right things, read all the books about nurturing and child-raising.

She had been the perfect PTA school mom, including

Girl Scouts and Boy Scouts. Nothing had worked. She couldn't understand. Marjorie had adored her parents, her friends, all her other relatives. But her two children, not so much. And there was nothing she could do about it now; she couldn't take them back to the store and exchange them for something she liked better or just drop them off at the Goodwill. Did any other parent feel this way, or was she the only one?

The sad truth was, she had just spent the last twenty-five years of her life waiting to experience the "joys of motherhood," and so far, she was still waiting.

She had realized long before Jim did that their son, Stanley, had grown up feeling the world owed him a living, and in fact was currently living off of them. As Jim used to joke, "I have an old seventy-eight-speed record player and a son down in the basement, and neither one of them works." From an early age, whenever it was suggested to Stanley that he might not be living up to his potential, his favorite retort was always "Hey, I didn't ask to be born." Sadly, he had a point. And even though he, at twenty-six, was now finally, technically, out of the house, they were still paying for his rent, food, and internet. It was a big expense each month, but Marjorie was secretly glad he had his own apartment. For the past five years, her entire house had smelled of marijuana.

Marjorie had watched her daughter, Betsy, grow into

what could only be called a phony. Being oh-so-sweet to other people but not to her family. Whenever she didn't get her way she would throw screaming fits and call Marjorie terrible names.

But Betsy had never been a happy child. And as hard as both her parents had tried to please her, they could never do enough or be enough. Just last year, they had spent a small fortune on her wedding, but she had complained all the way through it that her other girlfriends' weddings had been so much nicer. And the house she and Jim had bought the newlyweds was not big enough or grand enough to suit her.

The true worry Marjorie carried with her was that their unlikable behavior was somehow her fault. During their teenage years, she'd even gone to see a family counselor, telling him how much guilt she felt. He'd met with the children on several occasions and finally said to her that sometimes the child's behavior is not the parents' doing. "They can just come out of the egg a certain way, with certain personality traits." And yet, even after what he had said, Marjorie continued to feel like a failure as a mother.

Her only hope now was grandchildren. People said they were an awful lot of fun. So as disappointed as she was, she might have a second chance at motherhood.

And now, after waiting and hoping, her daughter had just called to announce that she was pregnant. And before Marjorie could start to celebrate the joyful news, her daughter was quick to add in her typical "poor me" tone: "And I just hope you'll be a better grandmother than you were a mother."

That night after the call, Marjorie cried herself to sleep. She realized her dream of becoming the loving grandmother of a loving grandchild was not going to happen either. Marjorie knew her daughter, and had been kidding herself to think she would ever allow a close relationship between her and that little unborn grandchild. And she knew that Stanley would never leave his computer games long enough to even date a girl, much less get married and have a home and children. It was a hopeless situation. And once again, she blamed herself.

After several weeks, she realized she was going to have to try and get over her disappointments, cut her losses, and somehow find a way to start over. But how?

It was Jim's idea. The next morning, Marjorie was actually excited as she drove across town, walked in the door of the local animal shelter, and announced to the redheaded lady behind the counter, "I'd like to adopt a dog please . . . no, make that two dogs. Oh, and a cat if you have one."

After filling out all the paperwork, she went home with one three-legged fox terrier, a ten-year-old cocker spaniel, and a little gray kitten with one eye, who purred every time you picked her up. After Marjorie left that day, the redheaded lady remarked to her coworker, "I'm so glad she took them. When she first came in, I could tell right away that she was a woman with a lot of love to give."

The Confession

Eddy and Timothy

Father Eddy O'Malley quietly snuck out of the rectory early that morning and drove across town to St. Anthony's Church. He wanted to make his confession before other people would be arriving. It was very important that he be the first one in the confessional booth. He had waited a long time to do this, and today was the day.

Father Timothy Shiel, the other young priest at St. Anthony's, was his friend, and both had come over to the States from Ireland. They had gone through the seminary together four years ago. He knew he could trust Father Shiel to never reveal what he would be confessing today.

Father O'Malley slipped inside the large, empty church and sat in the pew by the confessional booth and waited. At 7:30, his friend Father Shiel came in the side door and was adjusting his vestments when he looked up and saw his friend and smiled. But Father Eddy quickly bowed his head and did not make eye contact, which was unlike him. So, respecting this, Father

Timothy entered the confessional, and sat down and waited.

Father O'Malley went into the booth and began. "Bless me, Father, for I have sinned. It has been one week since my last confession," and he didn't wait for his friend to speak, but blurted out the sin before he had been asked. "Father, not only have I committed the sin of omission, I have broken my vow of chastity."

Father Timothy was taken aback. "Oh no, Eddy."

"Yes, Father."

"When did this happen?"

"Well, Mother Superior—Martha—and I have been secretly meeting for over a month now."

Father Timothy felt his jaw drop. "*Our* Mother Superior? Here at school?"

The young priest hung his head and whispered, "Yes . . ."

Father Timothy had heard a lot of shocking things in this booth over the years, but Mother Superior? She was a large and formidable woman at least twenty something years older than Eddy.

"And . . . where have these meetings taken place?"

"Different places . . . In the kitchen pantry, once in the vestment closet, but mostly in her room at the convent. Late at night. And then that one time, and I am so sorry for this, Father, in the back of your car . . . the one you loaned me . . . two weeks ago."

"Oh dear Jesus in heaven." Father Timothy prayed for

the right words. Eddy was his best friend; how could he have done such a thing? He'd always been so devoted to his calling. He felt the sweat running down his back. This was serious. It could mean dismissal for them both.

Father Timothy was searching for words when Father Eddy said, "But before you give me my penance . . . I have one more thing to say." Oh no, thought Father Timothy. He didn't want to hear any more sordid details about this affair. But he was a priest and was there to serve, and so he said, "Yes, what is it?"

Then Father Eddy shouted at him through the small door, "APRIL FOOL!!!!!! GOT YA!!!" and then got up and ran out of the confessional.

"What???" Then it suddenly hit Father Timothy. Today was April 1. Then he came flying out of the booth shouting, "You rat!!!! I'm gonna kill you. You scared me to death," at Father Eddy, who was now running down the aisle shouting, "Now we're even! Ha-ha!"

Father Timothy ran down the aisle after him, calling, "I'll get you for this."

When Mrs. Menelli, who was kneeling in a middle pew waiting to go to confession, saw her priest chasing another priest down the aisle and out the front door, she was startled. Wow, she thought. He must have confessed something pretty terrible. She was just here to confess that she had taken the Lord's name in vain when her dog had jumped up on the counter and was eating her lasagna.

After a moment Father Timothy came back in and now he was laughing. And when he saw her, he nodded. "Good morning Mrs. Menelli, I'll be right with you."

When she knelt down in the confessional, she could tell something pretty funny must have happened earlier, because Father Timothy kept suppressing a giggle all during her confession. And also he gave her only one Our Father and three Hail Marys to say. Usually she got at least one rosary, so he was still in a good mood over something.

She was right. Father Timothy was still laughing at what had just happened. Last year on April Fool's day he had put a pinch of itching powder underneath Father O'Malley's white collar right before he was to say High Mass. So yes, now they were even. But he had a whole year to plan what he would do next.

Although they were both devoted priests, and loved God with all their hearts, they were still young, and it was clear they had a little bit of the old Irish devil left in them.

A Thinking Man

Mr. Rushton Ingalls

Rushton Ingalls's parents had been quite bright, well-educated people. And right from the get-go, little Rushton had been informed that all human beings, himself included, had a time limit and would die one day. And to make matters worse, they couldn't tell him how many years he could count on. Just a ballpark figure would have helped.

Rushton often wished he had not been given this information at all. And at such an early age too. It had caused him a great deal of worry and anxiety. For instance, when he was younger, he had wondered whether he should work hard to try to make something out of himself or not. Why try, if life doesn't last? However, after a while, he weighed his odds of living a long life and decided to devote a lot of his younger years studying to become an electrical engineer, and eventually he landed a good job at a top firm. He figured that on the off chance he did make it to retirement age, he would certainly need the pension money and the Social Security that came with it.

Rushton's early hyperawareness of time passing had continued to interfere with his emotions his entire life. He could almost hear the ticking of the clock. Every time he said goodbye to someone, a part of him always wondered if it would be the last time he would ever see them. And if he was happy, he was all too aware that the happiness was only temporary, so he couldn't enjoy it as much as he felt he should. Rushton had spent his entire life waiting for the other shoe to drop.

For him, life had been like taking one long school test, wondering when the teacher would suddenly announce in a loud voice, "TIME'S UP!"

Even now, at ninety-two years old, Rushton had so many unanswered questions concerning time. Is time spent doing nothing really wasting time? And why do some people get more time than others? Why do some people take such a chance on shortening their time by doing such dangerous things? Why is time all we have? Why can't we stop time? Go forward in time or backward? That would be great, but sadly we humans are all at the mercy of that mean old thing called time. Time that always goes forward, never backward. Even those with millions of dollars to pay cannot buy even one more second.

Today, Rushton was sitting on a bench in the small park by his house and thinking that if he could somehow stop time, it would be when he first met his beautiful wife, and before his world changed. Before he became a lonely old man wondering why she was gone and he was still here.

Life was so mysterious. We all start out like bright-green little leaves, then one day wind up as a dried-up old brown leaf like him, just waiting to be blown away.

And finally after so many years of contemplation, Rushton came to a conclusion, and he quickly wrote it down on the back of his checkbook: "Sometimes it's a real pain in the ass to be a thinking person." And as he wrote it, he smiled, pleased at how wise he had become. But as he reread what he had just written, he suddenly started wondering something else: Why do some people go through life not thinking about things? Are they better off? Do they have more fun? Great. Now he was going to waste even more of his allotted time thinking about that.

His new conclusion about this was: Not only does time fly, nor time wait for no man, evidently, some things never change. Particularly me! He started to laugh, when suddenly, Rushton felt a sharp pain shooting across his chest. . . . As the pain continued, he broke out in a cold sweat. Oh no . . . this was it . . . the other shoe was now dropping. The moment he had been dreading all his life was finally here . . . his time was up! But wait . . . no . . . after Rushton had burped a few times the pain suddenly passed. Then he remembered those onions and peppers he had eaten earlier. It was not a fatal heart attack after all, just plain old indigestion. A false alarm. Hooraaaaay, he still had more time left!!! But why? So many of his friends hadn't made it to this age. How did he get so fortunate? And just how much longer did he have? And who or what was it deciding who goes when and who gets to stay? And why can't we decide when we want to go? It didn't seem fair.

Just then, a little dog trotted by his bench. The little dog, being a dog, had no idea that his life had a time limit and was living a perfectly happy life. Lucky dog!

Something to Look Forward To

Sigmond

SHENANDOAH, IOWA

2025

Sigmond Noodle wondered what the hell had just happened. A minute ago, he had been having lunch with his friends at the Motion Picture Retirement Home, and now, all of a sudden, he was sitting in a large field somewhere out in the country.

After racking his brain for over an hour, the only thing Sigmond could figure was that he must have just kicked the bucket. His doctor had warned him about his bad ticker. Yeah, that had to be it, he concluded. Geeeeez . . . what a bummer. And just when he had gotten a new knee too.

Sigmond had never believed in any of that silly reincarnation nonsense, but brother, had he been wrong, because here he was, no longer in his old body but some weird little puffy tan thing with six tiny legs!

Sigmond looked up and saw a grasshopper a few feet away and quickly called out to him, "Hey . . . hey you!"

The grasshopper looked over at him. "Me?"

"Yeah you, green guy. I need some help here, I'm confused . . . what the hell am I?"

The grasshopper said, "Hold on. Let me see," and hopped over for a closer look. After a moment he said, "Oh, you're a grub worm."

"A what? What the hell's a grub worm?"

"Don't you know?"

"No, I was raised in New York City, what do I know from grub worms?"

"Didn't you ever work in a garden?"

"Look, I was a publicity man for Warner Brothers Studio, we don't do gardener stuff."

"I see. Well, you're a grub worm now, buddy."

"A grub worm . . . huh . . . Go figure. Now, you ask me who's sleeping with who in Hollywood and I can tell you, but I don't have a clue what a grub worm is."

"Well . . . now you know."

Sigmond looked down again at his little fat body and moved his six little legs up and down and said, "Geez . . . I sure am one ugly-looking son of a bitch, aren't I."

The grasshopper nodded. "Yeah, you kinda are . . . Sorry, pal. Better luck next time." And he hopped away.

Sigmond sighed and wondered how his friends back at the Motion Picture Home were doing, and who would get his room. He hated that he had left so fast, with Morris still owing him that twenty-five bucks he won playing pinochle. Oh well, it is what it is. But then he started to wonder why he couldn't have been a grasshopper. That guy could really hop.

And so far, Sigmond couldn't do much of anything but crawl around a little and roll up in a ball.

After Sigmond had been out in the country for a few days, he was still having some trouble adjusting. The area where he had landed was jam-packed with hundreds of all kinds of different creatures, buzzing and scurrying and crawling all around. He had always heard that nature was supposed to be so quiet and serene, but this place was like Grand Central Station. The daytime was bad enough, but every night hundreds of lightning bugs and fireflies would swirl all around, winking and blinking, and he never dreamed nature was so damn loud! As soon as it got dark, all the crickets and the katydids and frogs would start up, making so much racket he could hardly sleep. Especially with that big loudmouth bullfrog over by the pond croaking all night long.

And one day, just as Sigmond was about to try to grab himself a little afternoon nap, a tiny ant jumped in front of him, wiggled his antennas, and said playfully, "Guess what I am!" Sigmond looked at him and knew what he was right away. He'd seen a lot of them running around his kitchen.

"No-brainer, pal. You're an ant."

"Aha," said the ant. "You are correct, sir. However, not just any plain old run-of-the-mill ant, but, get ready: a carpenter ant! And several lives ago, I was a giraffe! However, not on the great plains of Africa, as you might have guessed, but an American giraffe, born and bred at the San Diego Zoo. And you have no idea how amusing that was."

"No," Sigmond said but was sure the ant would tell him.

"Well, if you could have heard the things people said to me. Like 'How's the weather up there?' or 'We could use you on our basketball team.' Silly things like that. But you do learn how limited people are in conversation. So after a while, I was happy to move on. Oh, and by the way, every afternoon at four, we have a little discussion group that meets under the tree by the big log, and we'd be happy to have you join us. It's sort of a support group for those newcomers and old-timers who are having a hard time adjusting."

The last thing in the world Sigmond wanted to do was go to some meeting with a bunch of strange God-knows-whats. But he said, "Thanks for telling me, I'll think about it."

Later, after the chatty ant finally left, and just as Sigmond was about to get back to sleep, a small gray baby squirrel landed with a loud thud in the middle of a large pile of leaves right in front of him. The little squirrel crawled out and shook himself off. He then looked over at Sigmond and said, "Well, that was a whole lot of no fun. Man, I won't do that again. I just jumped off a twelve-story building in downtown Cincinnati."

Sigmond said, "Why would you do a fool thing like that?"

"I don't know, I guess that dude musta sold me something that had some bad stuff in it, because after a few snorts, I thought I could fly. Damn, that was stupid. I ain't no bird. I knew that right after I jumped, but it was too late." The squirrel looked around and said, "Hey, wait a minute. This ain't Cincinnati. This is weird . . . and why am I talking to . . . What are you, anyway?"

"Never mind," said Sigmond.

"And here's the funny thing. I'm not in any pain. You'd think I would be . . ." The squirrel suddenly looked down at his little paws. "Whoa . . . these aren't my hands, what's going on here?"

Sigmond said, "I'll make it simple for you. One word: reincarnation."

"You're kidding me, aren't you, bro?"

"Nope. You used to be a human, now you're a squirrel. Like I said, reincarnation."

"You're kidding."

"Nope. I was surprised too. But you might as well get used to it, because there's nothing you can do about it now."

"Well, I'll be dogged. A squirrel, huh? And here I

thought it was curtains for me, and instead I get another shot at it. How cool is that?" The squirrel turned around and looked behind him and said, "Hey, I've got a tail. And it curls . . . look at that!"

After he finished admiring his new fluffy tail, he said to Sigmond, "Hey, bro, have you seen any acorns around here? All of a sudden, I'm hungry."

"Try under that oak tree over there. I thought I saw a few lying around."

"Thanks. And thanks for the info. By the way, I'm Quentin. I used to be a side man. A studio musician. Now I'm Quentin the squirrel, I guess."

"Nice to meet you, Quentin. I'm Sigmond."

"Well, see you later, Sigmond," he said as he scurried off.

After the little squirrel left, Sigmond finally went back to sleep, but he was soon jarred awake again by the sound of a gopher rat from Portland named Mark, running by yelling, "Cat! . . . Cat! Cat! Run for your life!" Soon all the animals and birds were flying away and quickly climbing trees in a panic, scattering in all directions as fast as they could. Sigmond didn't know whether he should be scared or not. Do cats eat grub worms? He didn't know, but if they did, he was in big trouble.

He sure couldn't outrun a cat. So he scrunched down and sheltered in place and waited. A few seconds later, a large orange cat named Virgil passed by, and to Sigmond's horror, stopped and looked right at him and said, "Hey there, little fella, how you doing?"

Sigmond managed a weak little "Fine . . . you're not gonna eat me are you? I don't think I'd taste very good."

"Oh no. I'm just looking for birds or maybe rats. Seen any?"

"Naw . . . nothing around here like that."

"Oh well . . . have a good one!"

"You too!"

It had taken a few weeks for Sigmond to finally adjust to all the sounds, and he found that he was better off burrowing under the soft, loamy soil, where he could hear things that lived under the ground, too, moving and digging, but they were much quieter, and he was now able to sleep quite well, night or day.

One morning, Sigmond peeked his head out and was happy to see Quentin the squirrel, who had come by for a visit.

"So, Quentin, how're you doing, buddy?"

"Just great. You know, Sigmond, I've met some of the nicest creatures since I've been here. Why don't you come to that four-o'clock meeting with me sometime? It's a lot of fun, and you never know who might show up. You need to get out more. Meet your neighbors. It's not good for you to sit by yourself all day."

"Oh, I know," said Sigmond. "But I'm kinda embarrassed about how I look. I mean, who wants to look at a damn ugly grub worm? It's easy for you. You've got fur, and that tail . . . but . . . Naw . . . ."

Quentin looked at him and then said, "Sigmond, I want to tell you something as a friend. I think you're being way too hard on yourself about the grub-worm issue. You're a nice guy. That's all anybody cares about."

"Well, thanks, Quentin."

"I'll tell you what. Tomorrow, you and I will go together. Try it one time, and if you don't like it, then at least you tried, all right? See you tomorrow."

"Okay, but don't be surprised if nobody talks to me."

The next afternoon the two of them arrived at the small clearing, where all sorts of different creatures were gathered. Sigmond tried to sneak in and be as inconspicuous as possible, but wouldn't you know it, right before the meeting started that bigmouth ant announced in a loud voice, "Hey, everyone, let's give a great big welcome to Sigmond the grub worm." And of course, they all turned and looked at him and clapped their hands, or wings, or whatever it was they had. Geez, why did he have to say grub worm? Why couldn't he just call him by his name?

Then the ant continued, "Our topic for today's discussion is, 'Does size matter?' Sigmond, since you're new, would you like to start?"

Sigmond said, "No, I think I'll just listen today, thanks."

Quentin was right. Every creature who spoke had something interesting to say.

And there had been other surprises as well. During the meeting a small hawk landed right in the middle of the group and was very excited. "Hey, sorry to interrupt you guys, but I just have to tell you, I am so happy right now. You have no idea how great it is to be a hawk flying all around up there. When I was a human, I wore glasses all my life, blind as a bat, couldn't see three feet in front of me, and now I can see for miles. Up and down and sideways. My eyes are fantastic! And oh do I love having feathers! Everybody always said 'light as a feather,' and it's true. And they're so pretty too. Look," he said as he spread out his wings. "Well, gotta go, be seeing ya." And he flew away shouting as he went, "Yahoo!"

After the meeting was over, Sigmond had to admit that he had really enjoyed it, and he continued to go every day after that. And after a while, he even started joining in the conversations.

The next week the topic of the meeting was "Past Misconceptions of Reincarnation and Its Consequences."

"You know," a ladybug was saying, "I didn't believe in reincarnation, so I was not looking forward to dying, was scared about it really, but I must say this transition has been a wonderful experience. For me, at least." And everyone at the meeting agreed.

"It was a piece of cake," said a little skunk who used to be a legal secretary.

After a boll weevil shared his thoughts on the subject, Sigmond joined in by saying, "First of all I have to confess, I never believed in reincarnation either. I always thought it was a bunch of hooey. But what's funny to me now is that all the people I knew who really believed in reincarnation had it wrong. Oh, not that we don't come back. They got that right. It's just that they all believed they'd been Cleopatra."

They all laughed, including the small black spider on the rock. She didn't say anything, because she knew they wouldn't believe her, but she really had been Cleopatra, and she'd had a fear of snakes ever since.

Something over by the fence said, "I always believed in reincarnation, but I always thought I would come back as a person, not as a potato vine. So I was surprised, to say the least."

Just then a big fat possum waddled by on her way to the pond. Sigmond, who had never seen a possum in his life, was startled and whispered to Quentin, "Good God, what in the Sam Hill was that?"

"It was a possum," whispered Quentin.

"A what?"

"A possum."

An aphid chewing on a leaf, who had once been a science teacher in Denver, said, "Are you aware that an opossum, commonly called the possum, is the oldest living mammal on Earth?"

A small mosquito, who had just landed on Quentin's head, announced to the group, "Ladies and gentlemen, or what-have-you, permit me to interrupt. While it is true possums may live longer, believe it or not, it is I, the tiny mosquito, who is the most dangerous creature on Earth," he said smugly. "We, my fellow mosquitoes and I, have spread more disease and killed more people than any other living creature in the history of the world."

The ant stood up and said, "I think we're a little off subject here, and as for me . . ." He was going to say much more, but just then a little green lizard named Henry came running through the yard all upset and yelling at the top of his tiny lungs, "Look at this! I was minding my own business, not bothering anybody, when some damn crow flew down from out of nowhere and bit my whole tail off. Now what am I gonna do? I look terrible. And I had a date too!"

An owl with a sweet voice looked down from a tree and said, "Don't you worry, dear, you'll soon grow another one."

"Well, I just hope Janet doesn't dump me in the meantime."

The next time Quentin stopped by for his now-weekly visit with Sigmond, he was acting a little giddy. Sigmond looked at him and asked, "What's up? You're looking awfully happy today."

Quentin answered, "I feel happy. The truth is, I've met someone."

"Oh, you sly dog you. Who is she?"

"Her name is Doris, and she lives about six trees over. It looks like we might be moving in together."

"Wow, that was fast. Good for you, buddy."

"It is pretty great. And we have a lot in common, besides both being squirrels, I mean. She used to be a music teacher in Boston."

"Okay, well, it sounds like you got lucky."

"Yeah, Sigmond, I just wish you could meet somebody."

"That would be nice, but it looks like I'm the only grub worm here at the moment."

"Yeah, I haven't seen any others, but I could always fix you up with that possum if you want."

Sigmond looked at him and shook one of his little front legs at him and said, "You get outta here, you crazy guy, and you tell that Doris of yours I feel sorry for her if you're all she had to pick from."

Quentin laughed. "Okay, but in the meantime you take care, you hear?"

"I will. So long, pal. Good luck."

Sigmond was happy for him, but he would sure miss him.

. . .

The next week the ant announced the topic:

"The Pros and Cons of Being a Human Being versus All Other Living Creatures."

And Sigmond jumped right in. "Hey, listen, the only thing I miss about being human is baseball. Sometimes I wonder how the Yankees are doing, but that's it. They can keep the rest of it. What about you?" he asked a ferret.

"Oh, I wouldn't know, I've never been a human yet, just a rat and a pigeon. And a mouse once, but not for long. Walked right smack into that trap, first day."

"Well, that was rotten luck."

"Yeah, it was, but like I say, I've never been a human, but I'd sure like to try it sometime."

Sigmond said, "I wouldn't be in too much of a hurry if I were you, pal. Being a human ain't all it's cracked up to be."

"Yeah," said a little tan moth. "At first everybody is so happy to be a human, but they don't tell you all the stuff that goes with it. It's not as easy as it looks in the movies. Oh yes, you've got the love and sex thing, it can be a lot of fun, but boy, it can also cause a hell of a lot of trouble."

"Tell me about it," said Hazel the gopher. "Try being in labor for forty-eight hours in a covered wagon in 1846 with no drugs. Fun for you guys, maybe, not us girls."

"I agree with Hazel," added Agnes, a little brown

wren who used to be a waitress at a truck stop in Kalamazoo, Michigan. "Love caused me nothing but pain and heartbreak. Of course, when you're dealing with truckers . . ."

Joe the weasel, who once was a small-claims lawyer in Akron, Ohio, said, "Look, I was a human once. And don't get me wrong. I was happy to be alive. But what they also don't tell you is all the responsibilities that go with it, and how much trouble being a human really is. Just the maintenance alone is not only expensive but a pain. Think about it, all the stuff you have to do: brush your teeth, get your hair cut, clip your nails, eat three meals a day, put on your clothes, then take them off, go to school, get a job, then all the doctors you have to see, and the dentists, then all the pills you wind up taking, all the papers you have to fill out just to get Medicare, then you have to buy a casket and a cemetery plot. Nothing is free. And if you live a long time, it gets more and more expensive. At the end there, I got to where I couldn't afford myself anymore!"

"Well," said a little chipmunk, "everything you say is true, but I must say, when I was a human, even with all of its bumps and upsets, I enjoyed a lot of it."

"What?"

"Well, bowling, for one. I liked that. And my friends. I loved my friends."

Agnes the wren said, "I liked a lot of it too. But I think

having grandchildren was my favorite. They're so cute and fun to play with."

"You know what I loved best about being a human?" said the little ladybug. "Being wrong. I used to be so judgmental about everything and everybody. Then I realized it was great when I turned out to be completely wrong about somebody, or someplace."

Sigmond added, "Well, I'll tell you one thing. I don't want to be a human again, but if I ever am, I'll be a lot more careful where I step. One big, heavy foot can take out a lot of creatures."

A medium-sized pig sitting over in the corner said, "Well, if I'm ever a human again, I sure won't be over at the IHOP ordering any more bacon, I'll tell you that. Pancakes, yes. Bacon, no."

Later that afternoon, the whole yard was suddenly all a-twitter. The prettiest little gray mourning dove named Mary Lee had just arrived from Oxford, Mississippi, and was causing quite a stir. Sigmond didn't know if all doves were as pretty as she was, but this one was a knockout.

Sigmond said, "Honey, you sure are one good-looking bird, and I'll bet whatever you used to be, you were a good-looking one."

She batted her eyes and said shyly, in a sweet Southern accent, "You are so sweet to say that. Thank you." Then she glanced over at Sigmond. "I certainly don't mean to brag, but I was Miss Mississippi."

Whoa, thought Sigmond. He was right. Those Southern gals were all knockouts. Always in the top ten in Atlantic City. And you talk about lucky. Miss Mary Lee had gone from being a beautiful girl to being a beautiful bird. Damn. Just his luck. He had been ugly twice. Maybe there was something to that karma thing. Maybe he shouldn't have sold those stories about his clients to the *National Enquirer.* Oh well.

But then, he remembered the grasshopper *had* said "better luck next time," and according to the others, he should have a next time coming. So, at least he had something to look forward to. Sigmond sighed and wiggled underneath a leaf and closed his eyes, then started thinking about what he would like to be next. A lion, maybe? No. A shark? No. They have ugly teeth, and besides, he wanted to be something really cute. I know. A kitten. Yeah, a little fluffy kitten. And maybe some pretty woman would adopt me, and I wouldn't have to do a thing. Just eat and sleep, and sit in her lap, and be petted all day long. Yeah. A kitten. But not just any kitten. A Persian. Yeah. A little white Persian kitty with a cute little pink nose and little pink toes. Yeah, that would be perfect, he thought as he drifted off to sleep.

Sigmond didn't know it yet, but in just a very short while, he would be transforming into the cutest, perfectly formed little brown beetle, and all in the same lifetime.

In the meantime, a recent arrival, a little green turtle

named Patsy, sat happily sunning herself by the pond, just as calm and serene as she could be. When she had been a human, this had not been the case. For as long as she could remember, she had been on a constant roller-coaster ride of emotions. One day she was happy, and the next so depressed that she could hardly function. And the depression could last for many weeks or just an hour. She never knew from day to day. Her entire human life, she had been in a battle with herself. And at seventy-six, she had been just plain worn out and exhausted from the struggle. But as Patsy found out, sometimes pneumonia can be your friend. It had been for her. Now that she was here, for the first time she was no longer feeling those terrible ups and downs, only glorious, calming contentment. Oh, it was sheer heaven. And just now, a little bunny rabbit had happened by and stopped to chat. While they were talking, the bunny told Patsy how really lucky she was to be a turtle, because turtles live such long lives. What a relief to know that she had so many years ahead of her to just sit and relax, without a care in the world.

Patsy had loved meeting that happy little rabbit. She said her name was Velma and told Patsy the reason she was so happy. When she had been a human back in Kansas, she had always just loved bunnies, and now she got to be one.

Just then a tiny silvery fish jumped up out of the water and winked at Patsy. "Hey, cutie pie," he said.

"Hey, yourself," she replied, and winked back.

For the first time ever, Patsy was actually looking forward to the next day. And the next day, and the next. How wonderful.

THE END . . .

OR MAYBE NOT.

Regarding Special Agent William Frawley

Debbie

FORT WAYNE, INDIANA

PRESENT DAY

After the school crowd left the Baskin–Robbins ice-cream store, Debbie was behind the counter busy cleaning up when Phil, one of her regular customers, came in and ordered his hot-fudge sundae with nuts.

"Hey, Debbie, where's Bill Frawley these days?" he asked. "I haven't seen him around lately."

She sighed. "No . . . Bill's not here anymore; he was only in town for a short while on business. He said he had to get back and give some kind of report to his boss or something like that."

"Huh . . . Where's home?"

"I really don't know . . . all he told me was that he was from some little place I never heard of, but not nearly as pretty."

"Is he coming back?"

"No, I don't believe so."

"Well, that's too bad. I was thinking he was kinda sweet on you. I bet he hated to leave."

Debbie smiled. "Yeah, I think he did . . ."

Phil nodded and said, "Oh, and by the way, Debs, I like the way you're doing your hair now." Then he took a big bite of his sundae.

After Debbie got home that night, she fed the cat, kicked her shoes off, then sat down on the sofa, and began thinking. Life was so amazing, with all its strange twists and turns. You go along for years, then one day, completely out of the blue, Mr. William Frawley, a total stranger, walks in the door and hands you something you didn't even know you needed, and exactly when you needed it. After her husband had passed away and her son had married and moved away to start his new life, Debbie hadn't realized what her life had become. Just one dull routine after the other. Get up, eat breakfast, go to work, come home, feed the cat, watch *Shark Tank* or *Antiques Roadshow* on television, then go to bed. Then do the exact same thing the next day, with nothing to look forward to except getting older. But meeting Bill had changed everything.

First of all, she had not expected to ever feel excited over a man again. She had assumed that part of her life was over. And at her age, she had certainly not expected to have a man excited over her.

But from the moment they met, Bill made her feel attractive, and not only that, he seemed to find everything about her interesting and fascinating. The way she laughed, how she put on her makeup, just everything she did. And to top it off, he was adorable-looking. And she had surprised herself. She'd never invited a man to her home for dinner before, and at first was a little nervous about it, but after that first dinner she knew it would be okay.

Her cat, Mr. Tubbs, hated all men, and would hiss and spit at them and run under the couch whenever any man came into her house, including her own son, but the minute Bill walked in the door, Mr. Tubbs immediately ran over to him, sat down at his feet, and then rolled over on his back to be petted. It was almost embarrassing. He sort of made a fool of himself. Bill was the only man who had ever passed the cat test.

And not only was Bill cute, with those sparkly blue eyes of his, he was the most alive and most curious of human beings she had ever met, and certainly one of the friendliest. Whenever they went somewhere together, Bill would talk to everyone there, all about how they felt about this, or how they felt about that. And the man was never bored. He thought everything he saw was beautiful, herself included. He said he never saw such beautiful flowers, trees, and birds—all things she had stopped noticing long ago. And he loved to laugh. He thought it was so funny the way men chased a little white ball all over the golf course, cursing at it. And knock-knock jokes. He would practically fall on the floor laughing at them. And he loved going to different places. He even got her out to the zoo and the bowling alley. And Bill was so funny. As old as he was, he still didn't know how to drive a car. He walked everywhere he went. And he certainly never learned how to dance.

When she took him to a dance at the Elks Club, all he did was stand in one spot, shake his hips, and laugh.

Bill was just so different from any other person she had ever met. And he had such pretty teeth, too, and was always perfectly groomed with never a hair out of place, and skin as soft as a baby's. In fact, he looked like a big, cuddly doll, with the cutest giggle.

His enthusiasm and excitement over every little thing was contagious; it was so much fun seeing the world through his eyes. Soon her own outlook on life began to change.

Yes, Bill was gone and she would really miss him, but he'd left her with something she really needed: a new lease on life. And for the first time in years, she started waking up actually looking forward to the day.

Now men she had known for years started looking at her differently. When she looked at herself in the mirror, she even saw a new sparkle in her eye. She began to like the way she looked. She could see there was still life left in the old girl after all.

Yes, Bill was gone, but everybody who'd met him would not forget him. Even poor Mr. Tubbs still sat in the window looking for him. Debbie would miss him as well, but she was so grateful for the short time they'd had. And as to why she had been lucky enough to meet him? She didn't know. All she could figure was that he must have just been a gift from the universe.

Planet 8676

After the Break

Later, when Special Agent William Frawley returned to the Galactic Observer's Office to continue his report on his recent fact-finding trip to Planet Earth, the boss said, "So, tell me a little more about these humans."

"Well, sir, a lot of the humans are silly, but they can also be very brave. While I was there, I saw a man jump into a river to save another human's life. Somebody he didn't even know. But as I'd said before, many of the humans are very unhappy and don't seem to be enjoying themselves very much. And it's so sad, because there's so much there to enjoy."

His boss listened with great interest, then asked, "So having studied them up close, can you give a brief summary of what you believe to be their underlying problem?"

"Well, sir, like you said, humans are very complicated creatures, but having lived there for a while and observed how they operate, I believe that most of their troubles are caused by the fact that although humans are all the same species, they seem to want to separate into smaller groups. It appears to make them feel more safe and comfortable to be with other humans who think like they do and look like they do."

"Interesting."

"And no matter what happens, they all seem to blame it on the other group."

"What kinds of groups are we talking about?"

"Oh, all kinds. Religious groups, political groups, football groups, skin-color groups . . ."

"I see . . . Hold on a moment. Let me look this up."

After a few minutes the boss said, "Hmm. Well, scanning the history of humans from their beginning, I think I see what's causing the problem. It's a matter of evolution. Put simply, in some ways, humans may not be evolving as they should. Most are still following their primal tribal instincts."

"Their what?"

"It's a survival mechanism, coded into their DNA. As they were evolving into humans, they developed a natural instinct to gather together in tribes, for protection. So, as I see it, what was once needed to help them survive is causing them big problems now. And according to what I'm noting here, their weapons are no longer just sticks and stones but advanced nuclear weaponry. Also, the humans, as you have observed, have been quickly increasing their communication capacity and are likely on the cusp of colonizing other planets and, soon enough, entire galaxies. And this begins to be an area of concern for us. They'll have to straighten themselves out first before they start spreading their warlike behavior all over the universe, or before we know it, we will all be fighting each other, and we simply cannot let that happen."

"But how do we get them to stop fighting long enough to progress?"

"Good question." The boss did another quick scan. "I'm seeing that humans tend to do better when they bond together against a common enemy. For example, during two previous world wars they came together in two very large groups to fight against one another. But after the war was over, they began to separate back into their smaller groups, and these groups now seem to be dividing into smaller and smaller subgroups."

The boss thought for a moment. "Okay, so, here's a plan. If they don't straighten up in the next few Earth years, our Planet 8676 will initiate a war against their planet. Then, all the humans, all over Earth, will have to bond together to fight against us. See? In other words, every human on Earth will be on the same side, in the same tribe. Pretty good idea, don't you think?"

The special agent suddenly felt anxious. "Yes sir, but will we really go to war with them? I mean, they wouldn't stand a chance. We could wipe them out in a nanosecond. Should we go that far?"

"Oh no. We won't actually do it, we'll just threaten to annihilate them. Get all the humans to see us as their common enemy. Scare them into behaving themselves."

"And what if they don't?"

"We will cross that bridge if we come to it. But I wouldn't worry about that. If they don't come to their senses soon, humans are going to wipe themselves out anyhow."

The boss then shut down his screen and said, "So great job, Special Agent. Well done. I'm thinking there's a nice promotion in line for you."

"Thank you sir."

Later, back in his own cubicle, Special Agent William Frawley thought of how really fond he had grown of those silly humans and life on Earth. All like pretty birds and flowers. And the thought that they might destroy it all was very upsetting to him. There were some really nice people down there who didn't deserve to be blown up. They never did anything bad. His friend Debbie was one, and her cat. Although Mr. Tubbs did track kitty litter all over the house, he was still very sweet.

Then he started wondering what he could possibly tell the humans that might help stop all the fighting and bickering and yelling at each other, all the endless chatter night and day with neither side listening to what the other side was saying.

And after hours of thinking about it, Agent Frawley finally knew what he would say to the humans if he had the chance. He would simply say:

BE QUIET, PLEASE!

Epilogue

And so dear friends, I will take Special Agent Frawley's sage advice and be quiet. At least for now. But before I go, one last word regarding the human being. Considering all of the uncertainties and frailties that we humans have to face in life, we just may be the most courageous creatures that have ever lived. Because, in spite of it all, we just keep going. God bless us!

Fannie Flagg

Acknowledgments

A great big thank you to Kate Medina, my editor of many years—and all the great people of Random House Publishing—all my great agents at William Morris Endeavor, but most of all thanks to all the wonderful people who read my books!

About the Author

FANNIE FLAGG is a writer and an actress in television, films, and the theatre. She is the *New York Times* bestselling author of *Daisy Fay and the Miracle Man; Fried Green Tomatoes at the Whistle Stop Cafe; Welcome to the World, Baby Girl!; Standing in the Rainbow; A Redbird Christmas; Can't Wait to Get to Heaven; I Still Dream About You; The All-Girl Filling Station's Last Reunion; The Whole Town's Talking;* and *The Wonder Boy of Whistle Stop.* Flagg's script for the movie *Fried Green Tomatoes* was nominated for an Academy Award and for the Writers Guild of America Award and won the highly regarded USC Scripter Award for best screenplay of the year. She is the winner of the Harper Lee Prize, of which she is most proud.

About the Type

This book is set in Iowan Old Style. Designed by noted sign painter John Downer in 1991 and modeled after the types cut by Nicolas Jenson and Francesco Griffo in fifteenth-century Italy, it is a very readable typeface—sturdy-looking, open, and unfussy.